The Homecoming

The Homecoming

Louise M. Gouge

CROSSWAY BOOKS • WHEATON, ILLINOIS
A DIVISION OF GOOD NEWS PUBLISHERS

The Homecoming

Copyright © 1998 by Louise M. Gouge

Published by Crossway Books
        a division of Good News Publishers
        1300 Crescent Street
        Wheaton, Illinois 60187

All rights reserved. No part of this publication may be reproduced, stored in a retrieval system or transmitted in any form by any means, electronic, mechanical, photocopy, recording or otherwise, without the prior permission of the publisher, except as provided by USA copyright law.

Cover design: Cindy Kiple

Cover illustration: Laura Lakey

First printing, 1998

Printed in the United States of America

Library of Congress Cataloging-in-Publication Data
Gouge, Louise M. (Louise Myra), 1944-
   The homecoming / Louise M. Gouge.
     p.   cm.
   ISBN 0-89107-982-3
   I. Title.
PS3557.0839H66   1998
813'.54—dc21   97-32235

11	10	09	08	07	06	05	04	03	02	01	00	99	98
15	14	13	12	11	10	9	8	7	6	5	4	3	2	1

Dedication

To Ruth Cain Jacobs, my dear mother,
whose goodness and sweet temper
are always an example to me.

To Sue-Ellen Jacobs, my beloved sister,
who enriches my life with her wisdom.

To Beverly Slaughter, my mentor,
who won't let me quit learning.

To Karen Clark Stargardt, my friend,
who opened a magic door for me.

Thanks to all of you for believing in me!

Prologue

Ten years after Janice ran away from her unfaithful husband Bill "Buck" Mason, Janice was living with her son Billy and working as a waitress in a small Colorado town. Unexpectedly, Bill, now a famous quarterback for the Los Angeles Mavericks, came back into her life. He had, in fact, sought her out. Claiming that God had made him into a new man, he now wanted to make things right with his family.

Only after much questioning and a few crises did Janice even begin to trust her ex-husband's words and intentions. She listened to Bill, she allowed him to pay for an operation Billy needed for his bum leg, she hoped for the best. But just when pieces of the puzzle started to fit together, Bill sustained a critical injury in the most important football game of his career. Janice and Billy, who really shouldn't have been traveling anywhere only two weeks after his surgery, rushed to California to be with Bill, hoping for the best but having no idea what to expect.

JANICE AWOKE WITH A START. What was that loud thump?

"Hush, you two!" The sound of a woman's voice came through the bedroom door.

"But, Mommy . . ."

"I said, 'Hush.' Mrs. Mason is sleeping. Go play in your room."

Janice sat up in the bed, her memory quickly returning. This was Scott Lansing's home. Scott played on the same football team as Bill. The woman outside was Kate, Scott's wife, who had put an exhausted Janice to bed in the dark last night. Janice's ex-husband, Bill, was in the hospital, recovering from major surgery. And their son Billy was in the same hospital to ensure that his leg, in a brace since his recent surgery, hadn't been injured during last night's hasty plane trip from Colorado to Los Angeles. Was it only yesterday they had watched the football game in which Bill was so badly hurt that he nearly died?

As Janice pushed back the soft, fluffy comforter that covered her, she caressed its smooth fabric and traced its bright floral design, comparing it to her own pile of faded, well-worn blankets that never quite kept her warm in bitter cold Colorado winters. She glanced around the guest bedroom at all the matching decorations—curtains, overstuffed chair, throw pillows, and the dainty stool in front of the vanity table. Through the open door of the guest bathroom, she could see that even the towels matched the bedroom decor. She had been far too tired last night to notice or care. But in the light of day the obvious difference between her own low-income existence and the wealthy life of Bill and his friends made her feel more than a little out of place.

With a sigh she looked at the clock on the bedside table. Nine A.M.! She jumped out of bed, grabbed a quick shower, then dressed in jeans and a pullover shirt. She sat down at the large, ornate vanity mirror to brush her hair and dab on a little mascara. As she darkened her long blonde lashes, she frowned at her reflection. For years she had been content not to wear makeup. But since her ex-husband had come back into her life, she had become painfully aware of the glamorous women in his world, the world of professional football. With her pale skin, plain features, and long, straight, light brown hair, she wondered what on earth he saw in her.

Janice dug into her shabby, borrowed suitcase and found a pair of socks, then put them on along with her inexpensive tennis shoes. For a moment shyness held her back as she started to leave the room. But concern for Bill and Billy overcame her hesitation. Had her ex-husband and son slept as well as she had last night? She opened the door and walked down the hallway of the large suburban house, searching for Kate.

"Well, good morning, sleepyhead," the slender, bubbly redhead said as Janice entered the kitchen. "I was beginning to wonder if I should wake you. Coffee?"

"Yes, thank you."

Kate placed a steaming cup in front of her on the kitchen table.

The five-year-old twins, Amy and Sean, climbed on chairs and stared at Janice with impish grins. Their freckles and red hair matched their mother's. Amy was fine-boned like Kate, but Scott's tall, stocky build was already evident in Sean.

"Did you sleep all right?" Kate asked. She stood at the sink scrubbing carrots for the twins to munch.

"That's the most comfortable bed I've ever slept in." Janice thought of her own lumpy mattress on a steel frame in her bedroom back home. Yes, the bed had been comfortable, but now she felt quite *uncomfortable* in this large, beautiful house, so unlike her tiny trailer in southern Colorado.

"I called the hospital this morning." Kate brought her cup of coffee over to the table and sat down.

Janice gasped. "That should have been the first thing I did, even before I got dressed."

"Don't worry. Both your guys are fine. Buck, I mean Bill, had a rough night to begin with, but he settled down. And Billy's doing fine. Apparently all the nurses think the guys are so cute, they're fussing over them like crazy. I still can't get used to calling your hubby Bill. He'll always be Buck Mason to me—that's what all the players and coaches and fans call him. We can go to the hospital as soon as I fix you some breakfast. Scott's at practice. The team will have to work real hard to get their rookie quarterback, Joey Jones, up to speed so they can beat the Broncos next Sunday and win the American Football Conference championship," Kate said all in one breath.

Janice nodded politely, trying to grasp the significance of Kate's words. Her anxiety had decreased with the knowledge that Bill would recover and Billy was okay. But Bill's injuries were not merely a personal tragedy. The lives and careers of the entire Los Angeles Mavericks football team were affected— owners, coaches, players, even the players' wives and children.

"I guess the game is pretty important to everyone," she said, staring into her coffee.

"You bet. The guys have been working hard as mules. Buck, I mean Bill, is the best quarterback the Mavericks ever had. Even with him leading the team, it's taken them five years to get this far in the playoffs. Scott's been a receiver on the team for nine years, and he says nobody can put the ball in his hands like Buck. This year the team has really come together. But now without Buck . . . Jared Hammer didn't have to hit Buck that hard—and right in the stomach! He's walking meanness, that man. It's hard not to hate people like that!"

Kate stopped and glanced at her twins, who were staring at their mother. She quickly added, "Of course, the Lord wants us to forgive, no matter what. And injuries are just part of the game. Would you like some breakfast?"

"No, thanks," Janice said, sighing to catch her breath. Listening to Kate required a lot of energy.

Kate scrambled several eggs, prepared toast, and fried bacon in the microwave, then put out an array of jams and jellies. It wasn't until then that Janice realized Kate was as nervous to have her there as Janice was to be there. She ate a few bites of each dish to be polite, deciding that Kate shattered her image of the typical wife of a professional football player. Instead of being all glamour and poise, Kate was a regular person.

After clearing the dishes away, Kate ordered the children to put on their shoes and socks. "You're going to spend the day at Benji's house," she told them.

"Yay! Neato!" The twins squealed with delight, then scampered off to obey.

Kate grabbed a dust cloth and spun through the family room like a whirlwind, snatching up dust and clutter from every corner and cutting a swath through the jungle of toys the children had left. Janice picked up several toys and placed them in the corner toy box, then followed her hostess back to the kitchen.

"Where are you from, Kate?" she said, trying to make polite conversation.

"Kansas." The redhead tossed the dust cloth into the kitchen closet and smiled with satisfaction. "There! Now my husband will think I actually do some work around here! And you?"

"Oh, I have a job . . ."

"No, I mean, where are you from? But that's a silly thing to ask you. I already know you're from Colorado." Kate laughed at herself. "Well, come on, kids, let's go!" she said as the twins raced each other back into the kitchen.

After leaving the children at their friend's house, Kate drove her station wagon out of the Beverly Wood subdivision to the busy eight-lane Santa Monica Freeway. Janice stared out the window at the chaotic traffic, her heart pounding. Traffic in rural southern Colorado, or even in metropolitan Denver, was never this frantic.

As they drove, Janice enjoyed Kate's chatter, which covered topics from football to fashion. After a half-hour drive they exited the freeway and drove into an attractive development of professional buildings.

"That's the Cedars-Sinai Hospital," Kate said. "Do you recognize it in the daylight?"

"Not really," Janice said. "All I was thinking about last night was Bill. Aren't you going to stop?"

Kate shook her head and continued on past the building, finally parking in a shady spot a block from the hospital.

"Why so far away?" Janice asked. "I saw a parking lot . . ."

"What you didn't see were the sharks. Follow me." Kate removed a package from the back of her car, opened it, and handed Janice a white lab coat, then donned one herself.

"What's this all about?" Janice asked as she obediently put the coat over her clothes.

"We have to look like hospital personnel so we can get in without being stopped," Kate said.

"But we're allowed to visit . . ."

"You don't understand," Kate said. "All kinds of people will want to talk to you so they can get a story for their newspaper or tabloid. If you look like hospital staff, no one will know who you are."

"You're kidding . . . aren't you?"

"No, honey, I'm not. Welcome to the world of pro football. Next best thing to show biz."

Outside the hospital's main entrance, thirty or so people,

many holding cameras, were milling about, studying each person who approached the building. As the two women approached, Kate put on sunglasses, fluffed her long hair, and busily dug through her purse for a compact so she could check her appearance.

"We players' wives usually keep a low profile, but there's always a chance someone might recognize me as Scott's wife," she whispered to Janice.

Janice faced another shock when they got onto the appropriate ward and Kate explained that the men outside both Bill's and Billy's rooms were bodyguards. As Janice glanced into her son's room, the tall young man outside smiled and nodded.

"He's down in Buck's room," he said.

Janice's jumbled emotions calmed somewhat as she entered Bill's room. Twelve-year-old Billy was sitting in a wheelchair beside his father's bed, his left leg with attached stretching rod held up by the wheelchair's leg brace. His black hair was combed to match Bill's stylish wave, and their twin-like faces beamed at her.

A shiver raced down Janice's back at the sight of Bill's wounded body, with nasogastric tube and IV still attached. She swallowed hard to maintain her calm and put on a smiling face to match theirs.

"What a pair!" she said with a nervous laugh. "What are you two up to?"

She wanted to hug and kiss both her men, but adolescent Billy had rejected any physical show of affection for over a year, and her reconciliation with Bill was still new.

Kate had no such inhibitions. She marched across the room and squeezed Billy's shoulders, planting a big kiss on his cheek.

"Welcome to California, Billy! We've been praying for you for the longest time. How's your leg?" Before he could answer, she turned to Bill and gently kissed him. "You bum! Can't you even dodge a linebacker? Look at that pretty face of yours. Did you lose any teeth? I guess not. You've still got that gorgeous smile. Well, guys, I'm out of here. Janice, I'll be back to check on you in a couple of hours. Bye." Without waiting for a response, Kate marched out.

Janice watched her leave, then heaved a sigh. Bill chuckled softly, then pressed his abdomen to lessen the pain from his surgery.

"She wears you out, doesn't she?" he said.

"Yes. But she's nice. How are you two?" Janice studied Billy. His color was good and his face relaxed. "What did Dr. Bennett say about your leg?"

"She said I didn't mess it up by coming to California, but I need to stay off it. She didn't do any X-rays because she could tell it was okay. My left leg will be as long as my right one in a couple of months, and then I can start working out with Buck . . ." The boy turned toward his father. "I mean, with Dad."

Janice could see tears welling up in Bill's eyes at Billy's words, and she felt her own eyes stinging too. Had it really been only yesterday her son had wished his father dead because of the years of neglect? They had sat with friends in their small trailer in Colorado, watching Bill's football team play the Omaha Aces. One of the Aces, Jared Hammer, tackled Bill several times with illegal force, obviously trying to injure Bill. The final time he ruptured his spleen and nearly killed him. It took that horrible injury to persuade Billy to forgive Bill and to admit that he loved his father.

Billy squirmed in his wheelchair. All this emotion was too much for him. "Hey, Mike," he called to the young man at the door, "would you take me for a ride?"

"Sure, kid," the burly man said, crossing the room and spinning the wheelchair around a little faster than Janice liked. "Let's raid the snack shop."

As they disappeared through the door, Janice turned questioning eyes toward Bill.

"He'll be okay," Bill said. He laid back and closed his eyes. "How about you?"

He smiled a weary smile. "Guess I'm not too pretty to look at, am I?"

"You look awful," she said, smiling back at him, but also swallowing hard to keep from crying.

He chuckled softly, then frowned. "I have to ask you something. Last night, was it a dream or did you . . . did you say you'll marry me?"

"Do you really have to ask?"

"I just wanted to be sure I had it right . . . that this isn't some pity mission you've undertaken," he said.

"Bill, I wouldn't get in a tiny jet airplane for a hair-raising, late-night, thousand-mile flight if I were not very, very serious about where I was going and the man I was going to see. That was my very first and only airplane ride *ever*, and the only thing that got me through it was prayer."

His bright blue eyes sparkled. "Now you sound like Kate."

She giggled and returned his loving gaze.

"So, say it," he said.

"Say what?"

"That you'll marry me. Make it official. Wait . . . Let me ask again. Man, I wish I could get down on one knee." He frowned at the thought, then cheered up. "This will just have to do. Janice . . ." His eyes filled with tears again. "Will you marry me? Please?"

Janice blinked back the tears that sprang to her own eyes. "Yes, Bill Mason, alias 'Buck,' I will marry you. I would have told you two weeks ago when you came out to Colorado and brought Billy a computer for Christmas, but you left me in a cloud of dust."

He grimaced. "Oh, man. That long ago?" He rolled his head back and groaned. "Man, I sure have messed up my life."

"We've messed each other up," Janice said. "Now we have to put our family back together . . . with the Lord's help."

Bill gazed at her again, his eyes weary but loving. "That sounds mighty good to me. Why don't we start today?"

"Today? What's the hurry?"

"So you won't change your mind."

"Fat chance, mister. You're stuck with me."

"How about day after tomorrow then? Thursday at the latest. You and Kate can go get the license this afternoon."

"But shouldn't we wait . . ."

"Come on, Janice, live a little. Do something spontaneous."

Her heart seemed to beat faster at his challenge. "We have to ask Billy."

"I already did. He's all for it."

"Oh, Bill, I love you," Janice whispered. She leaned over his bed and gently kissed his forehead, wishing the tube didn't keep her away from his very appealing lips.

"Just one thing . . . don't tell anyone except Scott and Kate. The hospital staff is pretty good about protecting my privacy, but I'll have to give a press conference soon. Try to avoid the reporters, okay? If we let out that we're getting married, the place will be mobbed."

His words chilled her. She could just see the tabloid headlines: "Football Star Weds Small-Town Waitress." The memories of the crowd in front of the hospital, the bodyguards, and last night's ride from the airport in the team owner's limousine contrasted with her life in Colorado, reminding her of who she was and where she came from. It frightened her to think about entering such a different world.

"Sweetheart?" Bill's voice sounded weary.

"I'm here, Bill."

As he drifted off to sleep, she held his hand and caressed his cheek. How could she love him so much but fear his lifestyle? Could she cope with his world? How would Billy adjust? Did she even want him to? She pulled Bill's hand to her lips, feeling the power of his muscles even in repose. This was a very famous hand, known for throwing sixty-yard passes with little effort. But surely now, after almost dying, he'd hate football as much as she did. He'd want to settle down to a nice, quiet life, wouldn't he?

That was the answer, she decided. She would take him back to Colorado. They'd build a house and live happily ever after. How could he possibly object?

Two

HALF-AWAKE, BILL SAW a large shadowy figure pacing outside his hospital room, stopping several times to peer in at him. Bill tried to open his eyes all the way, but his eyelids wouldn't cooperate. Who was out there, and what did he want? Bill dozed for a moment, then awoke and felt more than saw the mystery man enter his room. He forced his eyes open just wide enough to recognize Jared Hammer.

Though a pleasant breeze flowed through the hospital hallways, beads of sweat clung to Hammer's brow and upper lip. His lean, massive, muscular body was in excellent shape, but he seemed to be struggling for breath, and his feet moved slowly as if weighted by gravity boots. He shuffled into the room and stood above Bill, an expression of revulsion on his face as he stared at the IVs and tubes.

"What am I doing here?" Hammer muttered, then turned to leave.

"Hey, man . . ." Bill croaked.

His weak voice seemed to jerk Hammer back like a marionette on a string.

"Come on in. Sit down," Bill said.

A rush of air burst from Hammer's lungs. "Uhh, I don't want to bother you . . ."

Bill grimaced as he tried to sit up. "Come on in, Hammer."

The burly linebacker sighed again, then pulled a chair next to the bed and straddled it, his arms folded across the back.

"I, uh, I . . ." he began.

Bill lay back, stifling a groan. "Thanks for coming. It's good to see you."

"Ha!" Another burst of air exploded from Hammer, followed by profanity. "Yeah, right. It's good to see me? Not! Go on, tell me you hate my guts for tearing into you like I did. Tell me to go to . . . to . . ."

His anguished crescendo ceased abruptly, and he put his forehead down on his arms. His shoulders heaved and trembled with silent sobs, and he was forced to jerk his head back up in order to breathe.

"I wasn't trying to kill you," he whispered hoarsely.

Bill's intense blue eyes held Hammer's. "I forgive you."

"Don't!" Hammer stood and shoved the chair against the wall, then stared out the window. The muscles in his jaw rippled, and he ran his hand through his dark wavy hair. Walking back to the bedside, he towered over Bill in an almost threatening manner, though the anguished expression on his face revealed anger toward himself. "Don't say that, man," he growled. "I can deal with you hating me. I can stand any revenge you try against me. Do anything you want. Say anything you want. Just don't say you forgive me. You *can't* forgive me. Because of me, you might never play football again!"

Bill winced at those words, but he smiled weakly. "But I do forgive you, Hammer. Jesus Christ loves you. And He forgives you too."

"No!" Hammer shouted. "Don't give me that . . . that garbage. There's no such thing as forgiveness!" He practically ran through the door.

Lord, help him understand, Bill prayed. Then he shuddered with relief. There was no telling what Hammer might have done to Bill, as upset as he was. Bill closed his eyes and groaned. The pain was still sharp despite medication, and this kind of emotional turmoil didn't help any.

Where was Janice? She and Billy should have been back from the hospital snack shop by now. They needed to begin making concrete plans about the wedding. Bill sighed, welcoming the sleep that enveloped him.

The vaguely familiar fragrance of expensive perfume and the gentle brush of fur against his bare arm woke him with a shock.

"Angela," he said weakly. "Angela Bains . . . It's been a long time."

A slender brunette leaned over him, her eyes moist. "Oh, Buck, my darling, I thought I'd never get in to see you! I was so frightened when I watched the game yesterday and saw you hurt so badly, I just had to come. Now I'm here, and I'm going to take such good care of you."

"Uhh, say, Angela, how about if I call you if I need anything?"

"Don't talk to me like we're strangers, Buck. I really mean I'm here to take care of you." The beautiful young woman caressed his face in a familiar way.

"Actually, I'm fine," Bill said. *O Lord, please don't let Janice see this.*

"Now, darling, don't try to get rid of me. You and I had a good thing going before you got so religious. Don't ever forget those sweet, special times. I really care for you. There's never been anyone in my life who has meant . . ." She stopped and followed Bill's anguished gaze toward the door.

Janice stood behind Billy's wheelchair, and mother and son both stared in disbelief as they recognized the famous actress leaning against Bill's bed with such familiarity.

"For heaven's sake, can't the staff keep the public out . . . Why, Buck, this little boy looks just like you. How adorable!"

"Angela," Bill struggled to explain, "this is my son, Billy. And this is his mother, Janice *Mason*."

"Wow!" Billy said. "Angela Bains! Can I have your autograph?"

Angela stared beyond the boy at her rival. "Oh, yes. Janet, isn't it? I remember you mentioning her. The ex-wife . . ." She tossed her long black hair back with a haughty pout, then forced a smile. "I see. It looks as though this was a wasted trip, darling. The role of nurse has obviously been filled. Oh, well, I never liked playing that part anyway." She gave Bill a quick Hollywood kiss. "Do take care, Buckie-Baby. We all love you, y' know. *Ciao!*"

She sailed out of the room with a theatrical flare, stopping beside Janice just long enough to give her a contemptuous once-over. "Take care of him, honey. He's one in a million."

As Janice watched the actress walk down the hall to the elevator, her stomach churned. Memories of reading about Bill in magazines and newspapers, frequently linked with women like Angela Bains, began to flash like neon signs. Jealousy raged in her heart, and she jerked about and fled to a distant waiting room, ignoring Bill's weak call.

For some time she sat angrily chewing her thumbnail, refusing to let the tears fall. How many other women had a claim to Bill's attention? Buckie-Baby indeed! What a thing for Billy to see! Marriage to Bill Mason would never work. They lived in different worlds, just as she'd thought.

Her anger was beginning to settle into bitter resignation when Dr. Miller, Bill's pastor, approached and sat on a nearby chair.

"Janice," he said softly, "how are you today?"

Janice nodded to the minister briefly, then looked down at her hands. Last night when Bill's life had been in jeopardy, she had appreciated his emotional support. Nevertheless, childhood memories of church made her distrust men like him. Unlike truck drivers and salesmen whom she could keep at arm's length with a smart remark, these men of God seemed to invade her privacy, trying to look deep into her soul. And that made her uncomfortable.

Dr. Miller went on, "I just spoke with Buck. He told me what happened. I can understand how you must feel, given all the details of your previous marriage and the destruction that Buck's infidelity caused. Forgive me for being blunt, but Buck and I have talked about this a great deal."

She stood up abruptly and walked to the window. Just exactly what had Bill told this man about her?

"Janice, in view of his high-profile profession, it's understandable that women he knew before he became a Christian are going to look him up now and then. But he is clearly committed to loving only you now."

Janice stared out the window at a young couple walking arm in arm along the sidewalk below. Their smiles revealed they thoroughly enjoyed being together. *One day they'll learn the truth about the illusion of love,* she thought bitterly. Turning to Dr. Miller, she said lightly, "Thanks for your concern. Everything is fine. Really." She only wished she believed it.

Dr. Miller sighed. "Well, you should probably tell that to Buck. He was pretty upset when you walked away. To go through this so soon after his surgery . . . Anyway, the doctor was called and . . ."

"Oh no!" Janice gasped. She rushed past Dr. Miller to return to Bill's room. What had she done! Last night she'd almost lost him forever, and now she was acting like a jealous teenager. She hurried to his room, where Billy still sat in his wheelchair, looking at his father with tears of worry in his eyes.

Dr. Joyce Bennett and two nurses were bent over Bill. Unable to see his face, she stood quietly in the doorway.

"Mom . . ." Billy said.

"What happened?" she whispered to her son.

"He . . . he got mad and pulled his IV out and tried to get out of bed when you left."

Janice felt guilty for refusing to listen to Bill. *Oh, God, please make him better.*

"Now you take it easy, young man," Dr. Bennett scolded as Bill lay flat on the bed looking pale and weary. "If another incident like this happens, I'm going to strap you into this bed and forbid any visitors!" The doctor marked Bill's chart, spoke briefly to the nurses, then walked out past Janice, directing a stern glance her way.

Janice meekly approached Bill's bed. His face reflected the pain he felt, and when he saw her, he closed his eyes and turned away. His jaw was set, but whether in pain or anger, she couldn't tell.

"Bill, I'm sorry . . . I . . ."

"Janice, about Angela . . ."

She took his hand and put it to her lips.

"It never happened," she said.

"But I . . ." he whispered.

"It never happened," she repeated firmly, then kissed her finger and laid it on his lips.

Janice returned to the Lansing home early that evening so Bill and Billy could rest. She called her dear friends Mac and Gracie Devine, owners and proprietors of a small diner back in Colorado, to let them know what had transpired since they'd all watched the football game together only the day before.

"We're going to get married Thursday at the hospital. Tell Alice and Frankie, okay? But nobody else." Their son Frankie and his wife had been a big part of what had been happening spiritually in Janice's life lately.

Janice listened politely as Gracie gave some unasked for advice. Mac and Gracie had been married for over thirty years. Though they seemed to bicker all the time, their eyes often reflected love. Janice could not bear the thought of ever arguing with Bill again.

After talking with Gracie, Janice called her mother in Alabama, apologizing for taking so long to let her know about Bill's condition. Margaret assured Janice she had been praying for her favorite quarterback without ceasing. When Janice told Margaret about the coming marriage, the older woman announced she'd come out on the first plane she could catch. "And this time I won't be drunk at your wedding, Janice."

"Mother, you don't need to say things like that. What's past is past."

"Maybe I don't need to say it for you, dear, but I do for myself. I can help you take care of Billy, too."

"Great. That prayer was answered before I even thought about it."

"The Bible tells us that before we call, God already has an answer waiting."

"Does it?" Janice asked. "Wow, God doesn't miss a thing, does He?"

Now she had two wonderful things to look forward to—her marriage and seeing her mother after ten years. She could hardly sleep that night, even in Kate's lovely guest room, as she anticipated the happiness awaiting her.

Bill brightened up when Dr. Miller returned to the hospital that evening. Though weak and a little depressed from the day's events, he wanted to make plans for the wedding.

"We want to get married here at the hospital on Thursday."

"Now, wait a minute, Buck," Dr. Miller said, "don't you think that's rushing it? You and Janice have a lot of things to work out before you remarry."

"Oh, we can work it all out as time goes by," Bill said. "The main thing is that we love each other. That will carry us through *any* problems."

Dr. Miller shook his head. "It would go so much better for you if you went through premarital counseling with me for several weeks, Buck. That way you can avoid some of those problems."

"We're both Christians now. We won't have any of the problems we had before. Besides, Billy shouldn't be moved back to Colorado before his leg heals. I'm getting out of the hospital in a few days, and I want Janice to move into my place right away so she can be there waiting for me. Everything will work out great—I just know it!" He didn't add that he was afraid Janice might back out. He *had* to get that ring on her hand soon.

Dr. Miller frowned. "Buck, I know you're both Christians, but that doesn't guarantee the best behavior or a harmonious relationship. You've only known the Lord for two years or so, and Janice was saved just a couple of months ago. You both have a lot of maturing to do. Don't you remember telling me that after you said your wedding vows the first time, your moral convictions gradually weakened and you began to behave badly? That can happen again despite your being Christians this time around. Both of you will have high expectations for the other person. Look at what you're putting Janice through right away—having to be a nurse to you and Billy. The honeymoon will be over before it even begins if you rush into this marriage without some serious counseling."

Bill smiled patiently at his pastor. "But since I do remember my old and very bad habits, I'll be sure to be on my guard. I really want to love and take care of my family."

Dr. Miller stood and walked to the window, staring out into the night. After a moment he turned to Bill. "You know, Buck, as much as I like football, it has always seemed a shame to me that most of the games are on Sunday. I'm not judging anybody, but we do miss seeing you at church. Tell me, how is your spiritual life going?"

The needles, tubes, and incision suddenly seemed to make Bill itch all over. He squirmed, trying to stop the discomfort. "I felt real close to the Lord just yesterday when I was . . . when I, you know, almost . . ." The pastor nodded in understanding. "I wanted to . . . well, go to be with Him."

"How do you feel today?"

"Oh, I'm glad to still be here."

"Yes, I can see that. But do you still feel close to the Lord?"

Bill shrugged. "Sure."

"Do you think you can lead Janice and Billy spiritually as the head of your home?"

"Sure!" he repeated, this time a little too forcefully. "I have it all planned. We'll have Bible study every day. Everything's working out for good—you know, like it says in Matthew chapter 8, verse 28."

"Romans chapter 8, verse 28?" Dr. Miller offered.

"There you go. Romans 8:28. It'll be great. Look at all the time I'll have to work on Billy to get him saved. Neither one of us can go anywhere!"

"But if you don't stay close to the Lord yourself, if things between you and Janice aren't all they should be, Billy will think you're a phony."

"Can you give me any scriptural reason why we shouldn't get married?" Bill asked, a hint of irritation creeping into his voice.

"No, I can't, none at all. I think you should marry Janice again. Just not so soon, and not until you have some counseling."

Bill lay quietly for a few moments, studying the ceiling. Then he gave Dr. Miller a pleasant smile. "Well, Janice and I are getting married Thursday morning here at the hospital, and we'd like you to perform the ceremony."

It was Dr. Miller's turn to be quiet for a moment. He finally sighed and shook his head. "All right, Buck. Against my better judgment, I will marry you and Janice this Thursday."

Three

"THIS IS THE MOST FUN I've had since I don't know when." Kate giggled as she stopped her sedan in front of the hospital.

Janice studied the marriage license in her lap, and her heart skipped a beat. "I still can't believe how easily we got away with it."

"I'm surprised the clerk didn't recognize Buck's name."

"People don't know him as William David Mason, or even Bill, do they?" Janice touched the names on the document, then shoved it into the safety of its manila envelope. Was this really happening? Were she and Bill getting married, or was she dreaming?

"He'll always be Buck to me. It really suits him, don't you think? And he's a maverick in more ways than one."

Surprised, Janice stared at her.

Kate looked back at her and blinked her eyes. "Oh, I don't mean anything bad. It's just that he has a mind of his own, and he's used to getting his own way. But he's a lot of fun and a great guy too. Look, hardly anybody's in front of the hospital, and the few there don't look like they'll be bothering you. But you'd still better wear the lab coat disguise. I'll pick you up at 4, okay?"

"Sure. Thanks, Kate." Janice gave her an uncertain nod and got out of the car. As she walked through the hospital door, a smiling young woman in a nurse's uniform fell in step beside her.

"Mrs. Mason?"

"Yes."

"Is it true that you and your ex-husband are getting married again?" She spoke in a confidential tone.

Janice smiled at the nurse. Happiness again bubbled inside her. "Well, I'm not supposed to say anything . . ."

"Janice!" Kate called from behind them.

Janice stopped. "Kate, I thought you were going home."

"I was until I saw . . . Well, let's go upstairs. You'll excuse us, won't you, dear?" Kate rudely brushed past the nurse and guided Janice into the elevator. When the other woman tried to follow, Kate said, "You'd better get out of here before I tell on you, sweetie. This is a private hospital, you know."

The elevator door slid shut, leaving an angry woman in white on the other side.

"Whew! That was close. What did you tell her?"

"Nothing. I didn't have a chance. Why did you do that?"

"Despite the uniform, that was no nurse. She's Roxanne Sumac, and she writes for a tabloid. She'll do anything for a story. When she doesn't get the facts, she makes things up based on her hunches. And her stories are always trashy. When Scott and I were having problems five years ago, she wrote some ugly things about us, and I'm sure she would have happily watched us get a divorce. Scandal sells, you know? The neat thing about it is, now that we're Christians, she thinks we're boring, so she leaves us alone."

As the elevator reached Bill's floor, Kate gave Janice a quick hug. "Beware of wolves in nurse's clothing, okay? See you tonight."

Janice had no time to recover before she was approached by a man in a business suit.

"Mrs. Mason? I'm Wilson, Buck's business manager. I have some papers for you to look over. Could we go into that waiting room over there?"

Janice glanced at him. Was this another reporter? "I really

don't have time," she said and pushed past him toward Bill's room.

"Mrs. Mason, may I explain . . ."

"Get lost!"

"Janice!" Bill called from his bed.

"Bill . . . I don't know what to do!" She rushed to his bedside for comfort. "A reporter in a nurse's uniform tried to question me, and now some man is following me. I'm sure he's not a doctor. He *says* he's your . . ."

"Business manager, which he *is*, Janice."

Color flooded her face, and the room suddenly felt hot. "Oh, I'm sorry . . ."

"Don't worry, I'll fix it. Wilson," Bill called to the perplexed man standing outside the room, "please come in."

"Mr. Wilson, I'm so sorry," Janice said.

"It's Hanson, Mrs. Mason. Wilson Hanson," he said with injured dignity.

Janice turned to Bill for moral support, but he just frowned at her. She lifted her chin slightly and looked back at the third party.

Clearing his throat, Wilson placed several papers on the edge of Bill's bed, then held one out to her. "This is the budget I've drawn up for you at Buck's request. Please look it over to be certain everything is satisfactory."

"What are you talking about?"

Bill exchanged looks with Wilson. "I'm sorry, honey. I never had a chance to explain to you . . . Wilson takes care of all my financial matters, so he'll be giving you your weekly allowance too."

"Allowance? You're kidding. Why can't you take care of your own money?"

"That's what I did my first year in pro football, and I ended up broke. With Wilson handling my money, I live on an allowance, and he pays my bills and invests the rest. Thanks to his financial management, I'm set for life, even if I never work again."

Janice refused to allow herself to cry. "Let me see it," she finally said as she reached for the paper.

"Here are your weekly expenses," Wilson said. "The personal ones, I mean. If this is satisfactory, I'll continue paying the bills for your condominium, your insurance, and . . ."

"Good grief!" Janice said.

"What's the matter, Mrs. Mason? Haven't I allowed enough?"

Janice kept staring at the paper. The weekly figure for her household budget was more than double what she made back home in a month, before taxes and including tips. A wave of the old bitterness surged through her. Life had been very hard for her, raising Billy alone on that meager salary, though her love for her son had made it worth any sacrifice. She couldn't begin to comprehend the figures on the paper before her. And to just have it handed to her every week . . .

"What do you expect me to do with all that money? And why do you have to set it up like some business deal? This is absurd . . ."

She started to turn and walk away, but Bill grasped her hand.

"Sweetheart, wait. You don't understand. It's not a business deal. We're just sharing everything. I have to live on a budget, and this is your share. How can that upset you?"

She refused to meet his gaze. This must be one of those prenuptial agreements she'd heard about. Was Bill just protecting all his money in case things didn't work out?

He tugged at her hand. She lifted her eyes to meet his icy blue ones, and he gave her his winsome smile. His face already looked better with that terrible tube gone from his nose and the scratches beginning to heal over. There were just enough bright red scars to remind her that she'd almost lost him forever. Reluctantly, she smiled. He had won her over again. But in the back of her mind she began searching for ways to earn her own money. It might be awkward for Bill if she were a waitress again, but maybe she could manage a restaurant. But then how would she take care of Billy?

She halfway listened as Wilson finished explaining the financial arrangements. She signed the papers and was glad when the man left. She decided to look on the positive side. At least now she could buy things for Billy. And it was good that Bill wanted to pay for his son's needs.

In the awkward silence that followed Wilson's departure, Bill held Janice's hand so she couldn't walk away. He wished he understood why she was so worried. Why all the fuss about signing the forms for her own checking account and credit cards? Couldn't she see that he was trying to do everything possible to make her happy?

"Sweetheart, what are you thinking?"

Janice bit her lower lip. *He doesn't trust me. He thinks I want his money. How can I prove I love him even if we have to live on peanut butter like we did when we were kids?*

"I got the license," she said, reaching for the envelope she had set on the end of his bed.

"Fantastic! Let me see . . ."

"Mrs. Mason?" A uniformed male nurse breezed into the room and set down his tray of medical supplies. "Could you please excuse us? We have some procedures to take care of. It'll only take a few minutes." He grasped the heavy white curtain and began to pull it around the bed.

Bill sighed with exasperation. "Don't go far, Jan. Okay?"

"I'll go see Billy." Janice gave him a quick kiss, then hurried down the hospital hallway to her son's room. She noticed with confusion and regret that she was relieved to leave Bill's side.

"Hi, Mom." Billy sat in his wheelchair, his left leg safely propped in its brace. "This is a cool computer game." He nodded toward the television and held up the control switch.

"Hey, sweetie. How's my big guy?" She bent down to kiss him but stopped when he wrinkled his nose and hunched his shoulders. With a sigh, she tousled his hair instead. "Would you like a break from conquering the universe? Let's take a ride."

"Cool," he said, switching the game off.

She wheeled him to the sundeck, hoping to enjoy the outof-doors, but a haze covered the sky, making them both long for the clean, clear air of Colorado. Janice felt a dull ache in her chest and knew it was from the smog. She wondered how long it would be before they could all move back to Colorado. Would it be hard to talk Bill into it? It would perhaps be best to convince him while he was still feeling weak. She shrugged off the thought that her tactic wasn't quite fair, deciding she would talk to him that afternoon, something that Bill's need for rest and Billy's busy chatter kept from happening.

That evening Janice and Kate met her mother at the airport, and her talk with Bill was postponed even further. But whenever she started thinking about the possible conflicts, she pictured his wonderful smile, remembered that she'd almost lost him forever, and assured herself that their love could handle any future problems.

Bill endured the pain as long as he could, then pressed the button on his medication control attached to the IV in his hand, allowing him to inject a doctor-prescribed amount of Demerol into his system as needed. Bill didn't want to risk using the painkiller too much. He'd seen friends become dependent on prescription drugs while recovering from severe injuries, then move on to illegal drugs.

As the medication began to ease the deep pain in his chest and abdomen, he was able to resume his former train of thought. He tried to concentrate on the answered prayers about winning Janice's and Billy's love back. He had prayed for a long time for his family, and now they were going to be his again. But couldn't God have found an easier way to get them back? Why did He have to take away the AFC championship and the Super Bowl? Bill knew his team could possibly win those games without him, but their chances were slim. There were a lot of good men on the team who deserved to win. They'd been working together for years, and this was their best season yet. They could've beaten Denver next Sunday and then played in their first Super Bowl. If only . . .

Pictures of Janice faded from his mind, and Bill imagined himself facing the Bronco defense. He saw Scott waiting downfield. He lifted his right arm to throw the ball, but the jerk of the IV brought him back to harsh reality. There would be no conference championship or Super Bowl this year. He felt a bitter ache rising in his chest. Maybe for him there would never even be another season. He wouldn't be the first to have career-ending injuries.

God, why are You doing this to me? Even as he thought the words, he knew it was at least partly his own fault that he was injured. Stupid, stubborn pride had kept him in the game against the Omaha Aces. The Mavericks had been winning 28-0, but he insisted on staying in the game so Billy wouldn't think he was afraid of the earlier threats made by Jared Hammer. If Bill "Buck" Mason's career was over, it was as much his fault as it was God's.

With Kate watching quietly, Janice and her mother sat beside each other in the airport restaurant, clasping hands. Neither seemed to know how to open the conversation.

After a few awkward minutes, Margaret began. "How does a person catch up on ten years of silent separation? How does a mother make up for her daughter's wasted childhood, years when all she . . . all *I* can remember is that you were a lovely, sweet girl growing up and changing into a woman . . . too quickly and too slowly . . . in a hazy, dreamlike way? Sometimes the guilt tears at my soul until I can't bear it."

Tears began to run down her cheeks, and she paused to dab them with a tissue. "I failed, Janice. I ruined my marriage and wasted my mothering years with you and Peter." Then she smiled and sighed. "But God has brought forth beauty from ashes. Look at you! Only God could make you the lovely person you are today."

Janice gazed at the well-groomed woman who sat beside her. Streaks of gray frosted the dark brown hair that stylishly framed her mother's slender face. "Oh, Mother, how could I have left you? I can't imagine the pain you must have felt all those years, not knowing where Billy and I were."

"But now we're together," Margaret said cheerfully. "Now we can be a family!"

"I love you, Mother."

"Oh, Janice, Janice, my dear, dear daughter, am I really touching you? I can hardly believe it!"

"You're such a beautiful lady, Mother. I wasn't even sure I would recognize you, but when I saw you come into the airport, I knew it was you."

"I would have known you anywhere. You've hardly changed at all. There's a healthy glow of love on your face. Oh, Janice, why did I run away from you and Peter? I could have done so much better."

"Mother, you didn't run away—I did."

"Oh, but I did too. What do you think drinking is? When I started, it was an occasional way of coping with the problems your father and I were having. After he left, I drank more to cope with the reality of our failed marriage. Before long, I was hooked. I was . . . I *am* an alcoholic. But now when I run, I run to the Lord instead of to the bottle."

Margaret paused for a moment. "Another thing that helps me is my family of Christian friends—people at church and others I've met. We all have the basic need of feeling that we belong. I never had that feeling as a child or in my marriage, and I certainly didn't give it to you and Peter. But I was finally found by a wonderful group of caring people. Through all my ups and downs, I can count on them to be there."

"You mean they accept you," Kate added.

"Oh, yes, Kate," Margaret said. "The Bible says we are accepted by God in His Beloved Son, the Lord Jesus Christ, and that's the way He wants us to accept and love one another. I was very blessed to find a church where the people could accept me as I was, because I was one messed-up woman."

Janice smiled uncertainly at her mother. She was glad she'd found a nice group of friends. But the thought of going to church didn't appeal to Janice. People could be awfully nosy at church.

"Darling, have you ever wondered about your father?" Margaret asked.

"Not much," Janice said. "I remember Peter telling me he probably died, and that's why you never talked about him while we were growing up . . . it made you too sad." She hesitated, remembering her mother's drunken tears whenever Janice would ask about her father. Having felt far less charitable toward their parents than her brother did, Janice had always figured their father had deserted them. But she wouldn't bring that up now. "I guess I've been too busy raising Billy to think about him." She paused again, frowning. "It never occurred to me before, but Billy and I both grew up without fathers. At least now Billy has *his* dad."

"Would you like to know about your father?"

Janice shrugged. "I guess so. You mean he didn't die?"

"Not as far as I know," Margaret said. "And I certainly hope not. But let me tell you about him. He was a very handsome man. He was quiet and had excellent manners. But he was a daydreamer and had a hard time keeping a job. He left shortly before I discovered I was expecting you."

"Didn't you try to find him then?" Janice said.

Margaret shrugged. "No. I was working at a pretty good job and was quite happy to be rid of him. At least I thought so. As the years went by, there just never seemed to be any good reason to reestablish contact, even when I lost my job . . . and even when Peter died. Of course, by then almost twenty years had passed . . . twenty years I barely remember."

She seemed lost in thought for a moment, but then she smiled. "Well, that's in the past. I needed to tell you these things, and I hope you'll feel free to ask any questions you might think of. But let's get on to happier things. When will I get to see Billy?"

So her father had abandoned them, just as Janice had always suspected. She stared at her mother. How could she speak of her husband's desertion so calmly? What a jerk he was to leave like that and never even let Margaret know where he was! But her mother seemed content to end the discussion, so Janice cheered up. After all, they were embarking on a happy new life for all of them.

"We'll go to the hospital first thing in the morning."

Wednesday passed quickly for Janice. She and Margaret visited Billy and Bill at the hospital, then went shopping for Janice's wedding dress. Janice preferred doing everything the simplest way possible and would have been happy to get married in jeans and a pullover shirt. But Margaret and Kate talked her into buying an attractive pink dress and pink shoes.

Thursday morning, the day of the wedding, Kate had a surprise for the excited bride. She had arranged for her hairdresser to come to her home and give Janice a makeover. The talented young woman trimmed and highlighted Janice's long hair, then styled it. She applied makeup so skillfully, Janice couldn't believe she was seeing her own reflection in the mirror. Rapt with excitement and anticipation, she allowed her mother and Kate to do everything for her.

When they arrived at Cedars-Sinai Hospital, they were pleased to find no fans or reporters awaiting them. Buck Mason's injuries were old news as people went on with their own lives. Die-hard Mavericks fans were now focused on their team, hoping they could pull together well enough to make a good showing in Sunday's playoff game against the Denver Broncos.

Bill awoke feeling elated at the prospect of being married to his beloved Janice. He regretted he wasn't yet able to eat solid food due to his surgery and the resulting weakened physical condition. By sheer willpower, he sat up and put on the loose-fitting blue dress shirt and the black tie and jacket he would wear for the wedding. He had to look good when she arrived, and more than enough female nurses volunteered to help him.

One by one people gathered in his hospital room: Dr. Miller to perform the ceremony, Dr. Bennett to keep an eye on her favorite patient, Billy to watch the reuniting of his parents, a trusted reporter and photographer to record the event, Scott to be best man, Kate to coordinate events, and Margaret to be her daughter's matron of honor. The adoring nurses had arranged the room with the flowers that had been sent for Bill, making it a makeshift wedding chapel.

Janice was a vision of loveliness, as all brides are. A mixture of excitement and numbness, she walked on a cloud toward Bill's room, her face glowing with joy. As she appeared in the doorway, a collective "Oooo" went out from the group.

Bill stared, wanting to be sure the right woman was entering his room. In all his love for her, in all the times he'd called her his beautiful Janice, he'd never dreamed she could look like this. Her long, straight hair had been transformed into a flattering frame of honey-blonde curls around her face. Skillfully applied makeup had erased the dark circles under her eyes. Her long lashes were enhanced by light mascara, and her cheeks glowed with faint blush and the reflection of the soft pink dress. How she'd changed from the pale, thin girl he'd searched for and found in that Colorado diner! She looked like an angel floating into his room to be his bride, and he suddenly felt more strong and alive than anytime since last Sunday's game.

The ceremony was brief and tearful. Janice hadn't even thought about a ring for Bill, and when he placed a beautiful diamond-covered wedding ring on her finger, she felt a moment of panic. To her great amazement and delight, Bill then reached out to Scott, who handed him a man's gold band—the very one she'd given Bill twelve years earlier when they married the first time. He had kept it all those years. Bill handed the ring to her, and she placed it on his finger and gently kissed him, not waiting for the pastor's permission.

Four

BILLY FOLDED HIS ARMS in disgust, trying to ignore the silly talk of his mother, his grandmother, and Mrs. Lansing. He had been released from the hospital after his parents' wedding, and he and his mother were on their way to Bill's condominium in the limousine provided by the Mavericks' owners. Billy had enjoyed the visits with his father every day and could hardly wait for his dad's release so they could recuperate together from their temporary disabilities. They had great plans for their future together.

The three women replayed the wedding to each other, giggling together over how romantically unconventional it had been. Janice was still amazed that Bill had kept his original wedding band, though he confessed that oversight rather than sentiment had prevented him from disposing of it. Janice wistfully thought of her matching band, probably sold long ago in the Alabama pawn shop where she had traded it for bus fare to carry her as far away from her cheating husband as possible. Now she studied the beautiful diamond ring Bill had given her today. Why didn't he understand she would have preferred a simple gold band to match his?

They arrived at the elegant Rosa Linda del Sol condominium complex built on a hillside in Beverly Hills. A uniformed doorman met them and helped bring in the few bags Janice and Billy possessed, along with Margaret's, who would be staying with them for a few days.

Janice tried to avoid staring at the opulent furnishings in the lobby, where another doorman led them to the elevator. The tall bodyguard who had stood outside Billy's door at the hospital now pushed the boy's wheelchair along the wide hallway. When the caravan arrived at the third-floor condominium, much to Janice's surprise, the door was opened by a pleasant, plainly dressed, middle-aged woman.

"Welcome, Mrs. Mason," she said. "I'm Mrs. Brown, Mr. Mason's housekeeper. I hope you will find everything in your new home to your satisfaction."

Janice looked questioningly at Kate.

"Oh, didn't you know?" Kate said. "Mrs. Brown has been with Buck for five years. She takes care of everything."

Janice had only a moment to wonder what other things Bill hadn't told her before she was ushered on into the living room. The scene struck her speechless. The room was large and elegant and distinctly male in decor. Her entire trailer would fill only a small corner of it. No wonder Bill had seemed so dismayed over her Colorado home.

Along one side of the room, oak wall units housed a large-screen television, video and compact disc systems, three separate aquariums, a variety of books, and artifacts of bronze, silver, and jade from various places where Bill had traveled. On the opposite wall, what had been a bar had been transformed into a soda fountain. Beyond the room was a patio that gave an extensive view of the city. A shiny black grand piano served as an informal room divider between the living room and the dining room. Luxuriant plants flowed over the sides of many planters, and several indoor trees were placed tastefully around the room.

Janice couldn't speak as she walked around the room, reviewing the elegance displayed in every corner. It was too much! Suddenly she wanted to grab Billy and run back to the simplicity of her home in Colorado. This place just wasn't her. It wasn't Billy. It wasn't even Bill, at least not the Bill she knew. Where was the simple taste he claimed to have? Why hadn't he given all this up when he became a Christian? It was more than luxurious—it was a monument to self-centeredness!

Unaware of Janice's struggles, Margaret and Kate were discussing various aspects of the beautiful condominium, and Billy was eating a banana split Mrs. Brown had prepared for him. Finally Margaret turned to her daughter and asked, "Honey, don't you think it's wonderful? How exciting to think of you living like this!"

"Well, it certainly will be a challenge to clean it," she responded lightly.

The other two women laughed.

"That's funny, Janice," Kate said. "Listen, with Mrs. B. around, you won't have to lift a finger."

Janice continued to survey the wonders of the condominium. Beyond the well-equipped kitchen was what seemed to be another apartment—a bedroom/sitting room with a private bath for Mrs. Brown. Beyond the main living room was a wide hallway that led to four large bedrooms, each with a private bath. In the master bedroom, the bath was entered by way of a dressing room with a big walk-in closet on one side and twin dressing tables on the other. The large oval bathtub was surrounded by luxurious houseplants, and controls on the wall above it indicated that the tub doubled as a Jacuzzi. Outside the bedroom was another patio, shielded by a redwood fence with a gate that, because the building was built on a hillside, led to an Olympic-sized swimming pool available for all the residents of the complex. To complete all the accessories a professional athlete might need, one bedroom had been transformed into a gym with an assortment of workout machines.

Janice was emotionally exhausted by the end of her tour. She was certain she had successfully appeared to like it, but her heart ached over the clash between her tastes and Bill's. This place was massive! She just wanted a small, cozy home. She wished they'd talked about it beforehand. Furthermore, there would never be any privacy with a housekeeper lurking about. She would have to go!

That night after she settled Billy into his new room and her mother was asleep in the guest room, Janice lay on a lounge chair on the patio overlooking the city. Although this suburb had less smog than some parts of the Los Angeles area, her weariness made the ache in her lungs worse, and once again she thought about Colorado. She had the sudden realization that Bill hadn't even implied he would go there to live. How would she convince him to leave this fancy condominium and enter her simple world? It wasn't that she expected him to live in the trailer. They could buy a nice, small home and live where the air was clean and the people homey and unsophisticated. They could have horses to ride, and she could have a big garden.

As she thought of all that Colorado offered, she grew calm, and for the first time in several days she prayed. *Lord, now that Bill won't be playing football anymore, help me convince him that we need to go back to Colorado.* Confident that God would answer this prayer as He had the others, she retired to the master bedroom and slept well that night.

Janice was thankful for Kate's willingness to take her wherever she needed to go. Janice had known few people she could trust: Mac and Gracie Devine, who owned the diner where she had worked for ten years; their son Frankie and his wife Alice; and Billy, of course. It seemed like all the other people she'd ever tried to trust had let her down. But Kate was kind and dependable, and Janice found herself believing in her friendship. Before her mother's arrival it had been fun to share the joy of her wedding plans with someone else. And now even though she and Billy had moved into the apartment, Kate was happy to drive her to the hospital to see Bill.

Janice had put aside the charade of the hospital lab coat. No one seemed interested in stopping her anymore, she thought the next day as she arrived to see her husband.

Husband! The thought of the word, the thought of the man to whom she was married, the thought of their being a real family, made her so happy she felt ready to burst. The day after the wedding, she could barely feel her feet touching the ground as she made her way to Bill's third-floor room.

She entered his room expecting to spend the day happily dreaming and planning the future with him but was quickly brought down to earth by the dark expression on his face. Rushing to his bedside and taking his hand in hers, she cried, "Bill, what's the matter?"

He sat propped against his pillow, almost glaring. "Janice, sweetheart, what did you do?"

"What do you mean?"

"Well, sweetheart . . ." The second use of that fond name with a twinge of irritation in his tone gave off ominous vibes. "My housekeeper just called. She quit, Janice. She's been with me for five years, and now she quits. What did you do?"

Janice stood looking at him in disbelief. Tears sprang to her eyes, and she bit back an angry retort. She started to turn and walk out of the room, but his hand tightened around hers. "You're not walking out on me." The look on her face was already making his anger fade. "Look, honey, I'm sorry, but Mrs. Brown has been with me forever. I can't get along without her. She does everything for me." His complaint trailed off, but he continued to hold her hand.

Janice stared beyond him at the wall, her chin set.

"Honey, I'm really sorry. I just want to know what happened. Janice, please talk to me."

She looked at him, unmoved by his winsome, boyish expression. After a moment she answered him quietly.

"You didn't tell me you had a housekeeper. This morning I got up and fixed breakfast for Mother and Billy. While I waited for Kate, I dusted the living room and watered the houseplants. I like to keep busy."

"Oh, that explains it." Bill laughed with relief. "It can all be straightened out. Honey, Mrs. Brown is hired to do the dusting and cooking. You hurt her pride when you did her jobs. It's like saying she wasn't doing her work properly. I'll call her and explain everything. It was hard enough to convince her to stay when I told her I was getting married, but . . . Never mind, I'm sure we can work it out."

"I thought when we got married, I would be taking care of your home—*our* home. I'm quite capable of doing that. That's the way normal people live. That's how Scott and Kate live."

"Sure, you're able to, sweetheart. I'm sorry. Honest. Will you please forgive me?"

His smile was calculated to make it impossible for her to stay angry, but she looked at him sadly, wondering what other unpleasant surprises she and Billy would encounter in their new life. All the joy of the morning had disappeared.

"Honey?" He tugged her hand. "I love you." He pulled her over for a kiss, but her foot slipped on the smooth floor, and she fell against his chest.

"Ahhh!" he cried in pain.

When she instinctively tried to regain her balance by pushing away, her hand pressed on his healing abdomen.

"Oh!" he groaned, doubling over in agony.

"Oh, Bill, I'm sorry. I slipped. Oh, dear, I'll go get the nurse."

"No . . . no . . . I'm okay." He pulled himself back up to a sitting position, breathing deeply.

"Bill, I'm sorry about your housekeeper. I didn't mean to cause a problem. Are you all right?" Janice couldn't believe she was apologizing to him when he was the one at fault. But he was hurt. How could she stay angry at such a moment?

"Yeah, I'm okay," he said, taking a deep breath and wiping the tears of pain from his eyes. After a few moments he recovered. "Look, could we please start all over again?"

"What do you mean?" Janice brushed away her own tears.

"I have an idea. You go back out the door and come back in with that sweet smile of yours, and I'll give you a proper greeting instead of my imitation of a grizzly bear, okay?"

"I'd feel stupid doing that."

"No, I mean it. Go on out. We have to try this again."

Janice looked at him for a moment, then turned to go out the door. Once in the corridor she waited several minutes, annoyed with both him and herself that she had actually apologized. It would serve him right if she went home. But when she heard him say, "Janice?" in an anxious tone, she couldn't bring herself to leave. Peeking around the door, she smiled impishly.

"Hey, mister, would you like a visitor?"

"Yeah, I sure would," he said, sighing with relief. She hadn't left after all.

She walked over to his bedside to give him a quick, gentle kiss, but he reached up and pulled her closer for a longer one. "That's better," he said in her ear.

She tried to pull away. "I'm afraid I'll hurt you again."

"I'll let you know if you do." He started to kiss her again, but the nurse came in to announce it was time for him to take a walk.

As they ambled along the corridor, Bill leaned on a cane with his left hand and used Janice's shoulder as a resting place for his right arm, still sore from having an IV needle in it for several days. He was afraid his weight was too great for her, but she assured him she was stronger than she looked. She hadn't been sitting on a pillow and eating bonbons for the past ten years!

Bill greeted patients and hospital staff enthusiastically. His presence on the floor caused excitement for those not used to seeing him, and he enjoyed the attention. Janice was growing accustomed to his notoriety and was deep in thought about other things as he visited with other patients.

She wondered again how she could get him to move out of the condominium. Even with two spacious patios, it was no place for Billy to live, all cooped up, with no real outdoors. And there was still the matter of the housekeeper. They hadn't really solved what had caused their argument. They had just swept it all aside when Bill got hurt. She was enjoying the happy moments too much to bring up anything that might upset either of them. Everything would work out once Bill felt better. She was sure of it.

Saturday came and went peacefully. As they spent their time strolling the hospital corridors and sitting on the sundeck, Janice was certain her earlier concern had been in vain. Bill was easy to talk to and was agreeable about almost everything. She wondered if he would want the two of them to study the Bible together. She had a ton of questions she wanted to ask him. He didn't seem to be talking about God like he had before. She'd meant to bring him his Bible from his bedside table but had forgotten. She decided to put off the subject until later, though she did manage to bring up another idea close to her heart.

"If you could only taste the delicious barbecue beef and delicious baked beans Frankie cooks at the diner! They're out of this world! Mac and Gracie have worked real hard over the years, but because of the fancier restaurants and fast-food chains, they've never been able to do more than just get by. If someone could invest in a new building and equipment, they could start a barbecue pit that would bring people all the way from Denver." Of course they would need her to organize the operation, but she didn't mention that yet.

"That sounds like a good idea. I really appreciate their taking care of you and Billy all those years I didn't. Maybe such an investment would be a good way to say thanks."

Janice went home Saturday evening feeling confident that soon she could present the second phase of her dream: getting them all back to Colorado. She promised she would be in Bill's room at 1 P.M. the next day to watch the playoff game between the L.A. Mavericks and the Denver Broncos, but she didn't understand why he was even interested in seeing it. Wasn't he through with football after almost being killed by it?

Kate was unable to drive Janice to the hospital on Sunday. The game promised to be the most exciting one of the season, and she had gone to watch it in person. Billy still needed to avoid moving his leg any more than necessary, so he and his grandmother stayed home to watch the event on television. The new experience of taking a taxicab alone made Janice a bit nervous. However, after a little help from her mother and the doorman, she was on her way only slightly behind schedule.

As she approached Bill's room, she heard several voices and the blaring television. Peeking around the corner, she was surprised to find half a dozen people or more watching Bill watch the game. A television camera was focused on him, and a man with a microphone stood by recording Bill's comments. Janice had missed the kickoff by fifteen minutes, so the game was well under way. She drew back from the room unnoticed, trying to figure out what was happening. Why were these people recording Bill's reactions to the game? Janice found herself backing down the hall in confusion.

Bill, on the other hand, was used to being watched. After five seasons in professional football, he could be himself with no nervous thoughts about the 60,000 fans watching in the stands or the millions watching via television. But this time instead of watching him display his skill on the football field, television viewers would be scrutinizing his emotions and expressions as he watched his team play without him. Since becoming a Christian, he had with God's help mastered his temper on the playing field. But recently he'd felt himself drifting into a growing estrangement from the Lord, and he wondered if he could watch the game without doing or saying something that would be a bad example for the many people watching him. Man, did he want to be out there! Where was Janice? He wanted her by his side!

The contest between the two evenly matched teams ebbed and flowed. For every hard-won Mavericks touchdown, the Broncos scored one of their own, and both defensive teams made the opposing offense work hard for whatever points they could manage. Rookie quarterback Joey Jones was performing well, and Bill watched with pride as his protégé executed plays that he himself had helped design. The kid was coming along great, and although Bill really expected the Broncos to win, he was glad his young teammate was making such a good showing.

Janice sat in the hospital's main lobby, where several patients were watching the game. Occasionally doctors, nurses, and other personnel would stop by to check the score. Janice could see that the game was going to be close and knew how happy that would make Billy, who was surely rooting for his dad's team but also supported the team from their home state. When the broadcast cut away to Bill to check his reactions, he looked as though he wasn't missing her at all. She was glad she hadn't gone into the room. As the game progressed, only her desire to see Bill on TV kept her watching.

In the closing minute of the final quarter, Joey Jones made a daring quarterback sneak into the end zone, pushing the Mavericks' score even with the Broncos. The extra point attempt was successful, giving the Mavericks a 35-34 lead. The Broncos were unable to score in the little time remaining, and the game was over. The Los Angeles Mavericks had won the American Football Conference championship—their first!

Bill's on-camera, post-game excitement frightened Janice. *He shouldn't be bouncing around like that! He'll hurt himself!*

The sports commentator was saying, "And so, folks, rookie Joey Jones steps out of the shadow of the great Buck Mason and leads his team to victory with a strength and maturity seldom seen in rookies. It took Buck Mason three years to develop that kind of skill and daring on the playing field. Jim, what's happening there in Buck's hospital room?"

"Well, Buck, what do you have to say?"

It took Bill a moment to recover from the earlier commentator's cutting remarks, but he managed to comment. "Great game! Joey was great, the team was great! What can I say? Denver deserves a lot of credit—they're a great team, but this was our day. Go Mavericks!" Bill let out a whoop for emphasis, and the picture went back to the stadium, where thousands of fans poured onto the field and carried Mavericks coach Chuck Speer off the field alongside Joey Jones and Scott Lansing. Scott had set a record for the number of catches in a playoff game and had been named MVP.

Janice didn't understand what it all meant, but she was happy for Kate. She sat in the lobby until she saw the television crew leave, then ventured upstairs, wondering what to expect. Would Bill be angry? His door was closed, and his room was dark as she tiptoed in. He seemed to be sleeping, but as she approached his bedside, she could see the set of his jaw and the furrowed look on his brow.

"Does it hurt?" she whispered, her heart warming at his obvious misery.

He opened his eyes slowly, and the haunted expression in them made her heart ache for him. "I should've been there, Jan. I should've been there. It was my own fault . . ."

"Oh, Bill, I'm so sorry." Sorry for his hurt. Sorry for his emotional pain. But not sorry for his being out of football. How could he still want to be there? "It'll be okay. It'll work out."

He held her hand, pressing it to his lips for comfort, nodding to try to make her words true. Then he looked at her and asked weakly, "Where were you? I missed you. I kept looking out the door hoping you'd come. Is Billy okay?"

Janice could not meet his gaze. "I . . . I saw the crowd and figured there wasn't any room for me."

"Oh, sweetheart, there'll always be room for you, wherever I am. I'll make room for you. You and Billy are what really count to me. I can't wait to get home so we can start living like a family."

Janice sighed with relief. He had his mind on the right things now.

Five

LIKE A PREDATOR watching for prey, Bill eyed every person who walked past his room. *When is Dr. Bennett coming? She should've been here hours ago*, he complained to himself even though it was only a little before 8 in the morning. He hoped to convince her he could go home today. She was hard to fool, but maybe if he smiled a lot, he could win her over.

Finally the tall, gray-haired woman marched into his room in her usual almost military fashion and began reviewing his chart.

"So, what mischief have you been up to since yesterday, Buck?"

"What could I do in here?" He smiled winningly at her.

"Uh-oh, I can tell by that look that you want something. I suppose you think you're ready to go home?"

"I feel great! Eight days in this place is plenty for me. I'm ready to go surfing." His eyes twinkled.

"Well, you won't be doing that for a while . . ." she said absently as she studied his chart.

"Okay, Mom." He deliberately used the Mavericks' nickname for their favorite doctor. "Let's have it. I want to know everything."

She frowned, then sat on the side of his bed, removed her glasses, and stared into his eyes. "Buck, how did your father die?"

"My father? Uh, well, it was a plane crash. Small plane . . . he and my mother . . ."

"Don't play games with me, Buck. How did he die?"

"Well . . . the autopsy revealed a heart attack. I wasn't surprised really. He'd had heart trouble . . . you know, rheumatic fever as a kid and all that. What are you thinking? I've never had any trouble with my heart . . . unless you count my divorce." He grinned at her, then frowned. "Dr. Joyce, what's going on? I'll play football again next season, won't I? I know I'll be okay by then."

Dr. Bennett patted his hand. "I won't lie to you, Buck. We're going to watch your heart rhythms. There may have been some complications during surgery . . . Subsequent testing revealed some irregularities. For now, it all depends on you. You'll have to slow down for a while. Your surgery wasn't routine like having your tonsils out. You won't heal properly without restricting your activities for several weeks, then gradually working your way back with the team's personal trainer. No excessive excitement. Just relax. Sit around the house and watch TV reruns for a while. Just concentrate on getting well."

Bill sighed with relief. "You had me scared for a while, Doc. You really had me going. I'll be good. I promise."

"So do you want to go home today?"

"Do I!" he exclaimed, starting to bolt out of bed, then catching himself.

"Now that's just what I'm talking about, Buck! You're more of an adolescent than your son. You need to take lessons from him in how to sit still. I'm going to give Janice a strict set of rules for you to follow, and you'd better mind her, you hear me?"

"Yes, ma'am," he said, giving her a charming smile as she rose to leave. Man, would he be glad to get out of this place!

"Oh, by the way, Doc," he added as an afterthought, "can I go to church next Sunday?" He owed that much to Dr. Miller for giving in and performing the wedding.

"I don't want you to drive for another four to six weeks," she said. "But if someone else takes you, it will be all right."

"Great!" He swung his legs over the side of the bed and began organizing his things.

"Remember, Buck. Four to six weeks of proper rest. Have you got that?"

"Yes, ma'am." He grinned at her and winked.

Dr. Bennett shook her head but smiled back and pointed a finger at him. "If you don't do what I tell you, I'm going to tell my big brother Ryan—owner of the Mavericks, I'm sure you remember him—to be very good to Joey Jones when contract time comes around."

"Ouch! Yes, ma'am!" Bill said, feigning a lighthearted response. But her joke struck a tender nerve.

That afternoon was filled with bustling activity and mixed emotions. Many of Bill's teammates and their wives were at the condominium for his homecoming. Balloons, streamers, and a large *welcome home* banner decorated the living room.

There was much ado as Bill came through the door walking with his cane, but at least walking. Everyone cheered, and a celebration began that lasted for the rest of the afternoon.

Janice had relied on Kate once again, this time to obtain refreshments for her guests. But as she served them, she thought back to the diner in Colorado. For the most part, she found the men here to be much like the truck drivers she'd waited on for ten years. They weren't as fresh as the lonely truckers because in most cases their wives were with them. But then again they were louder and more boisterous.

High spirits reigned because of the championship conquest the day before, and everyone included Bill as a part of the winning team. After all, he had brought them to the playoffs.

Joey Jones was an interesting young man to watch. From the first moment Janice saw him, he seemed to be testing who was in charge. In many ways he looked to Bill for approval for his performance the previous day. In other ways, he seemed anxious to unseat Bill from the center of attention. It was obvious to her that he was an outrageous flirt and that he was full of himself for the way he'd come through for the team.

Billy sat on one of the large couches in the cavernous living room. His left leg, with its steel stretching rod, was carefully propped up, and his eyes took in all the excitement. Janice was busy with the guests, but she was sure she served him two sundaes from the fountain. *Oh dear, he'll be sick tonight*, she thought when she saw him eating a third. But she had to hurry to the kitchen right then and had no time to scold him. Anyway, he was having so much fun with all these famous athletes, each of whose football stats he could recite from memory, that she couldn't deny him any of the pleasure of the experience.

Several times during the party Kate tried to involve Janice in conversation with the other wives, but Janice managed to avoid prolonged chats. She had nothing in common with these women, she reasoned, and would not be seeing them again. It was easier for her to make sure that the food kept coming and leave the chitchat to Kate.

Mixed with Janice's and Billy's happiness at Bill's homecoming was the regret that Margaret would return home to Alabama that very day. Her promise to visit on her next vacation made the parting a little easier. As the guests began to leave, Margaret said a few words of encouragement to Bill, kissed her daughter and grandson good-bye, then left with Scott and Kate for the airport.

Janice worried as she settled Billy in bed that evening. His eyes danced with excitement as he repeated conversations he'd had with the various members of the team. While Janice was grateful for the attention the men had given her son, she feared the physical consequences of the day's events. Billy confessed to having consumed four sundaes and three hot dogs, so Janice put an empty plastic trash can by his bed and a glass of water just in case.

Next she made sure Bill was settled comfortably in the king-size bed in the master bedroom, then went to prepare for bed herself. She put on the beautiful negligee her mother had given her as a wedding gift, then brushed her long hair. She'd sleep in the guest room tonight, so she wouldn't risk bumping into Bill during the night and hurting him again. Gathering her clothes, she went to say good night to Bill.

"Wow!" he said. "You look fantastic! Come over here."

She went to his bedside and smiled. "Now you lie still like Dr. Bennett said and get a good night's sleep. I'm going to be in the guest room, but I'm a light sleeper, and I'll hear if you call me."

"Don't be silly. This is a huge bed. There's room for both of us." He pulled her onto the bed and began to run his hands through her hair. "Hmmm, silky. Janice . . . my sweet wife Janice. You're so beautiful." He drew her close and kissed her.

She gently pushed him away and pretended to scold him. "What do you think you're doing?"

"I'm kissing my wife." He pulled her back and whispered in her ear.

Pleasant shivers raced down her back. "But aren't you exhausted and sore?"

"I'm feeling noooo pain," he murmured as he began to kiss her neck.

"Mo-o-m!" Billy's faint call came through the door.

"Oh, Billy needs me." She carefully pushed against Bill's shoulders and stood up, trying to regain her composure. "I'll be right back."

Ignoring Bill's frown, she hurried down the hall, then stopped to quiet her racing heart before entering Billy's room.

He had accidentally pushed his water glass out of reach. After putting the glass closer and giving him a kiss despite his objections, she went back to the master bedroom.

Ducking in quickly, she grabbed her clothes from the chaise lounge where she had left them. "Well, I'm off to the guest room. Sleep well . . ."

"Janice, you get over here right now or I'm coming after you." He threw the covers aside and started to place a foot on the floor.

"No, don't do that!" she cried. Dropping her bundle, she rushed toward him, stopping within a yard of the bed.

"All the way over here."

"But . . ."

"Janice, come here," he said gently. He held out his hand.

She laid her hand on his and sat on the edge of the bed.

He slipped his arm around her and pulled her close, stroking her hair. "My sweet angel, I love you so much. Stay here with me. Just to be close."

Janice felt a warm glow filling her. "It feels so good to have you hold me."

Without warning, Bill pulled her across his body, landing her on the opposite side of the bed. She squealed and laughed in surprise as she rolled over to look at him. But his hand was on his bandaged abdomen, and his jaw was set, fighting the pain.

"Oh, I knew it," she cried. "Why did you do that!"

"I'll be okay," he said through clenched teeth. "Just give me a minute." He took a deep breath, then forced a smile. "There. That's better. Now where were we? Oh, yeah. Come here."

She lay stiff in his arms, afraid any movement would further hurt him.

Bill switched off the lamp, and as her eyes grew accustomed to the dark, Janice studied his face. He seemed past the pain, and she was finally able to relax into the pleasantness of being close to him. In all her years of loneliness, she'd never imagined feeling so safe, so warm, so cozy. And she had never imagined so much happiness.

Six

THE DISAGREEMENT over Mrs. Brown was temporarily resolved when Bill sent the woman on a paid vacation. He had been able to convince her that she would surely be needed by the end of the month and also promised a raise when she returned.

Janice, on the other hand, was certain that she could prove herself capable of caring for their home and nursing her two men back to health at the same time. She tried to be lighthearted when talking to Bill about it, but in her deepest feelings she couldn't bear the thought of another woman hovering over her in her own home. She could do her own work and do it well.

Although the condominium was large, it was easy to care for. The smooth oak wall units dusted easily, and the shiny bathrooms cleaned quickly. Janice admitted to herself that it was more than pleasant not to have holes in the walls and raggedy carpet that needed to be sewn together from time to time like in her trailer. She felt she was keeping up with her work quite well as she established a daily routine for the family.

"There's only one problem with this place," she told Bill one day. "As fancy as it is, it really should be a little more stable. Every time a heavy truck goes by, the whole building shakes."

Bill chuckled, then winked at Billy. The two had been playing a video game while Janice dusted the living room. "Umm, no trucks are allowed on this street, Jan. Those are . . . shall I say, 'earth movements'?"

Janice stopped dusting and stared at him. "Earth movements? You mean *earthquakes?*"

"Sure. It's no big deal. This is southern California, remember?"

"Yeah, Mom," Billy echoed. "This is southern California."

"Right," Janice said, then returned to her dusting. *No big deal? We're all going to slide into the ocean, and it's no big deal? Oh, God, please get us back to Colorado soon!*

To do her grocery shopping, Janice took a cab to the shopping center a half-mile from the condominium. One of the helpful doormen told her that most residents simply ordered their groceries by phone. But she rejected that idea, preferring to walk up and down the grocery store aisles, able for the first time in her life to buy whatever she wished. She had to admit that having money gave her many advantages. She also discovered the fun of creative cooking and took pleasure in giving Billy all the fruit and healthy snacks he wanted.

Bill watched her with delight. He felt proud of being able to provide for his loved ones. Each day as he and Billy parked themselves in the living room for another day of television, video games, and talk, he thought about ways to make life better for them.

He decided that Janice needed more freedom of mobility in her shopping so she wouldn't be forced to take a cab or call Kate for a ride. So one afternoon he announced that he would start giving Janice driving lessons the next day.

"Driving lessons!" she said. "Bill, if I wouldn't drive on the country roads of Colorado, what on earth makes you think I'd want to drive out here with all these crazy people?"

"I'll teach you. It'll be easy. We'll start in the morning." His tone was kind but firm. The subject was closed.

The following morning, after settling Billy in the living room, they began the project.

"You can do it, Mom!" Billy said, giving her a thumbs-up sign.

Janice looked at him doubtfully. "If we're not back in an hour, call Kate." She placed the phone on the table beside him.

"Aw, come on, sweetheart, this will be easy. My car practically drives itself. Billy, give us three hours. Once your mother catches on, she won't want to stop." He winked at his grinning son as they left.

In the basement garage Bill introduced Janice to Walter, who took care of the residents' cars. Then he showed her his shiny metallic-blue sports car, which typified everything Janice had come to expect of Bill.

Once again, she puzzled over the fact that though he was a Christian, Bill made sure he had the best of everything. That contradicted earlier claims of simple tastes. But rather than stir up an argument, she filed the information for future reference.

She was still looking for ways out of this frightful project as he seated her behind the wheel, then limped around the car, shoving his cane into the backseat.

"Oh, I just thought of something," she said over the lump of fear in her throat. "Don't I need to get a learning permit of some kind first?"

"No problem," he said with only a slight twinge of conscience. "With my expert teaching, you can skip right over that and get your regular license in no time. Now listen carefully . . . This is the steering wheel . . ."

She giggled nervously.

"This is what you hold to steer, okay?"

"Really? What's this?" She turned the radio on, and the loud blare of music filled the small car. Bill reached over to turn it off.

"That's called a distraction. Now this is the gearshift." He pointed to the stick shift on the floor. "Say 'gearshift.'"

"Four on the floor?"

"No, it's automatic. Now let's get serious. You put the key in the ignition . . . No, wait, I need to tell you something. That's the brake right there. That's important because if all else fails, you stomp on that and get out and let me drive."

"Bill, this is so stupid. We should wait. You can't drive. Dr. Bennett says your recovery depends on your not doing anything foolish."

"I was just kidding. Don't worry, you're going to do fine. Now put the key in. That's right. Push the accelerator. Turn the key. Good."

The car started with a loud roar. "Not so much gas. Okay, now put the car in reverse... That's the R there... Right." The car began to roll backward down the slight incline of the garage floor.

"Look behind you, and turn the wheel to the left... Left! Janice, left! Put on the brake!"

But her foot went to the accelerator instead, and the car jerked backwards. Quickly she slammed on the brake, and as the tires screeched on the concrete floor, they were both thrown forward. Janice stared ahead, gripping the steering wheel, her foot firmly on the brake.

"I don't think I can do this," she whispered.

"Sure, you can." Bill held his right hand on his aching abdomen. "But I did forget one important thing... seat belts. Put on your seat belt. Good. Now put the car in drive... that's the D with the circle around it... and slowly, *slowly* press the gas as you turn the wheel back to the right."

The car moved toward the entrance of the garage where a short, steep incline led down to the street. To Janice it looked like the brink of a bottomless pit. Her eyes were wide as she put the brake on, jerking the car as they coasted down the driveway a little at a time.

She allowed the car to come to rest in the street at the bottom of the incline. Rosa Linda del Sol Parkway was not a busy street, and at the moment their path was clear. Janice gently pushed the gas, and the car inched smoothly forward.

"Okay, now pick up a little speed," Bill said.

She obeyed. He had been right. The car almost did drive itself.

After several minutes of moving slowly along the straight street, Bill told her to put on the blinker for a right turn. She flipped the lever on the side of the steering wheel, but to her amazement the windshield wipers came on.

"No, sweetheart, the other one."

Janice quickly flipped the other lever. But by then she had passed the street where he'd wanted her to turn.

"That's okay," he said. "Just turn at the next street."

That was an unfortunate choice. Traffic moved quickly in both directions as they approached busy Wilshire Boulevard. Janice came to a complete stop at the stop sign, losing whatever confidence she'd gained.

"I can't drive out there."

"Sure, you can. Look how far you've brought us already."

A knot of fear lodged in Janice's throat as she watched for an opening in the oncoming traffic. Bill watched, too, and soon became impatient with her hesitation.

"Go, honey! You can make it. Go!"

"No, I can't!"

"There's an opening. Go for it!"

Wincing at his tone of voice, she mashed the gas pedal, squealing the tires as she turned the wheel sharply to make the right turn. But not knowing how little pressure the power steering needed, she caused the car to swerve too far to the right.

"Turn it back the other way!" Bill shouted.

It was too late, and as she tried to compensate for the mistake, she sideswiped a parked car.

"Brake it! Brake it!" Bill shouted.

But again she hit the gas by mistake. The car shot across traffic, narrowly missing an oncoming truck, and raced into a parking lot. Janice hit the brake pedal and screeched to a halt only inches from another vehicle.

Gripping the wheel, Janice stared straight ahead. As relief replaced terror, her mind seemed blank, unable to comprehend Bill's terse instructions.

"Get out and come around to this side. Hurry!" He shoved her toward the left door, then pulled himself out of the right and leaned on his cane.

Janice numbly followed his orders as he studied the scratched and dented side of his pride and joy.

"Look what you did to my car!" he snapped. But seeing people begin to gather around them, he quickly recovered. "I was driving, okay, Janice? Nobody saw us."

"But . . ."

"Don't argue with me!" he hissed.

Fortunately, both the police officer who came to investigate the accident and the owner of the damaged car were die-hard Mavericks fans. They expressed concern over the star quarterback's driving too soon after being released from the hospital, but each seemed more eager to share his own reactions to the game in which Bill was injured than to worry about today's little incident. Of course, Bill received a citation for careless driving, but he took it with good humor. Everyone knew Buck Mason was a good guy, and to prove it he spent several minutes signing autographs for the policeman and the crowd that had gathered. Bill seemed so charming and contrite, the other man came away feeling almost privileged to have had his car hit by this famous athlete. It was a story he could tell his grandchildren.

Janice and Bill took a taxi home from the driving lesson and sent Walter to retrieve the damaged sports car. Throughout the rest of the day, they maintained a polite exterior for Billy's sake. But he was bright enough to see that things hadn't gone well. Hoping to cheer them up, he spent the afternoon challenging Bill to video games and, at dinner, chattering about television shows and complimenting his mother's casserole.

That night Janice lay in frozen silence on the far side of the king-size bed. Her shock and hurt over Bill's behavior had grown to anger, then turned to depression.

On the other side of the bed, Bill turned his back toward Janice and frowned into the darkness. How could anyone not know how

to drive? He pictured the badly scraped and dented side of his car
. . . the dream car he'd had specially designed and equipped. But as
the digital clock radio on his bedside table gently clicked away
moment after moment, hour after hour, his feelings began to soften.

Things are different now, he thought. *I have a family. I need to
redesign my life a little. Maybe I should buy a different car . . . a family
car . . . maybe a van like Scott's.*

Then it hit him. He'd sent her into the game without a game
plan. He'd set her at the wheel expecting her to know things she
obviously didn't. It wasn't her fault she'd never learned to drive.
Today was more his fault than hers. How could he make things
right? She was very quiet, lying as far as she could from him and
still be on the bed.

"Helloooo," he whispered. There was silence.

"Sometimes a king-size bed seems a lot bigger than it actually is. It feels like the Grand Canyon tonight."

No answer.

"Maybe tomorrow I'll buy a double bed."

Still quiet.

"Two singles?"

He wondered if he should roll over and kiss her good night
and see what happened. But the accident had strained him, and
a dull throb in his abdomen reminded him how tired he was.
He'd have to wait until morning.

Janice was glad he stopped. One more remark and she would
have giggled. It was impossible not to forgive Bill when he
became contrite. But she figured she had to give him a dose of
silence to punish him for his unreasonable behavior. Blaming
her for the accident he made her have! She'd fix him a terrific
breakfast to let him know that all was forgiven.

In the morning, as Janice was preparing a Mexican omelette
for Bill, the door chimes rang. A delivery man handed her a large

arrangement of three dozen pink roses and baby's breath in a white wicker basket. While he was placing it on the glass dining room table, another delivery man entered with a large, ornately wrapped package. On his heels was a third man with a smaller package. All were for Janice.

Her eyes were wide as she opened the large box and discovered a white fur coat. She gently caressed the shiny fur, then pulled it out, revealing its full length.

Where would I ever wear this? she wondered, laying it back on the box. She opened the smaller box and found a glistening pearl necklace. She stood in front of the buffet mirror and put the pearls around her neck, covering the simple heart pendant Bill had given her. *It's not me. My gold heart is all the jewelry I want.*

As she turned to take the coat from its box once more, she saw Bill, leaning on his cane and watching her with a crooked, boyish grin.

"You didn't have to do this." She walked over to him, and he pulled her close.

"I wanted to say I'm sorry for yesterday. Do you like them?"

"They're beautiful. All of them." She looked at him with concern. There was a weariness in his eyes.

"Bill, do you feel all right?"

"I'm a little tired. Didn't sleep too well last night." He held her close, smelling the fragrance of her freshly washed hair. "Will you forgive me?"

"You don't have to buy me things for me to forgive you."

"I know. But when I treat you badly, I want to make up for it."

"How on earth did you get these things ordered so early?" she asked. "A florist might be open this early, but the coat and the necklace . . ."

"You just have to know the right people. With the right name, a person can get whatever he wants, whenever he wants it, with just a phone call." He smiled with self-satisfaction that his name carried that kind of power.

"Oh." She was confused by the uneasiness that Bill's words caused within her. "What kind of fur is this?" she asked, trying to quiet her thoughts. She tried the coat on and gazed at herself in the mirror again.

"Mink. Every woman's dream, right?" He smiled. She looked great in his gift.

"Well . . ." she began, then stopped.

"Well, what? Is there something you'd like better?"

She shrugged. "I don't know what it would be. It's just that some winters when I walked to work in 40 below zero weather, all I wore was a jean jacket." She frowned. Now they were in southern California where she didn't even need a warm coat.

"Didn't you ever dream about having better things?" He came over to the mirror and pulled her into his arms again.

"I was never much of a dreamer. I just worked."

"Well, start dreaming now. You can have whatever you want in this world."

She buried her face in his chest for a moment, then looked up with misty eyes. She wanted to tell him that something deep inside her resented being Cinderella, but no words would come. How could she share what she herself didn't understand?

Bill smiled down at her. "I'm gonna buy you the moon, sweetheart, and we're gonna fly there." Before she could respond, he kissed her gently, then firmly, pulling her against him. Janice answered his kiss warmly as the hollow ache in her heart softened. She felt almost smothered in his embrace, then realized it was the coat!

"Oh, Bill," she gasped, pulling back, "I'm roasting."

"I thought I smelled fire," he said, chuckling.

"Your omelette!" she cried, breaking away from him and dashing to the kitchen.

Seven

JANICE SETTLED HERSELF next to Bill in Scott's van, looking out the window and worrying about leaving Billy alone for several hours. She had thought of a dozen excuses for not going to church, but once again Bill had proven himself able to talk her into anything.

The trip to church went too quickly with the twins chattering happily and making the adults laugh at their five-year-old view of life. Janice had developed a great affection for the children and was almost beginning to enjoy the ride when they arrived at Pleasant Hills Community Church.

It was an attractive building with an A-line front. Although fairly new, it was already bursting at the seams, and a new building was under construction on the left side of the main sanctuary. On the right side, the Sunday school annex beckoned them as people flocked in, chatting and waving to friends, making the place seem homey and welcoming. Scott and Kate disappeared to their respective teaching responsibilities.

Janice thought about her mother's church and how they had welcomed the alcoholic woman and changed her life. *Maybe these people will be okay,* she thought. *I'll really try to give them a chance.* She looked up at Bill as they walked toward the building from the parking lot and wondered why he seemed a little nervous. Was he afraid she would embarrass him?

Bill leaned on his cane as he walked, a little more than necessary. Though he wouldn't admit it to anyone else, he was uncomfortable about going back to church. There were certain people he'd have to avoid close contact with—the ones who would ask him how things were and really wanted to know. He had to appear as though everything was fine.

Sunday school proved to be pleasant enough. Many friends spoke to Bill, and he introduced Janice to the class, taking attention off himself. As the lesson began, Bill felt a strange warming in his heart as he showed Janice the appropriate verses in a borrowed Bible. His eyes misted over at one point when she looked up and smiled at him, just as she had done the night in her trailer when she trusted the Lord Jesus as her Savior. What had gone wrong? He was supposed to be teaching her about the Lord, and yet they hadn't even opened the Bible once since they got married. He'd even forgotten to bring his Bible to church!

The church sanctuary was not as large as Janice had imagined, and as it began filling with people, she could understand why they needed to expand the building. But the thing she noticed most was the warm atmosphere among the people. Not only did friends visit with each other between services, but visitors were made to feel at home. Bill was welcomed back by various acquaintances, and each person made some pleasant remark to Janice. Several young women looked at her appraisingly, and she wondered with a moment of subtle jealousy how many had tried to win Bill's affection. But they were polite to her, and she found herself enjoying this new experience.

Just moments before the service began, a handsome, well-dressed couple about their age approached and chatted with Bill. The friendly eyes of the young woman found Janice's, and she smiled warmly.

"So you're from Colorado," she bubbled. "Tell me, which do you prefer, Aspen or Vail? We're looking for a new place to go skiing, and Buck can tell you that after a while Mammoth and Sun Valley get boring. Have you tried those state-of-the art lifts at Vail? I hear they're terrific. Oh, the choir's coming in. I'll catch you after church. We're so happy for you and Buck!" She smiled over her shoulder as her husband guided her away to find a seat.

All the happiness that Janice had been allowing herself to feel disappeared in those few seconds the skiing enthusiast had spoken to her. So Bill skied too. And now everyone would assume that she knew everything about the sport that was so important to Colorado's tourist image. Where would she have ever found time or money to ski, even if she'd wanted to? Once again she felt inadequate to be part of Bill's world.

But even as her heart was sinking in self-pity, the music began, and though she still felt uneasy, the strains of the opening anthem lifted her spirits. The large choir overflowed the loft at the front of the church. But the singers' joyful faces impressed Janice even more than their number. The song was one she'd never heard, and she was surprised at the modern beat.

Okay, she thought, *let's try this again. I will enjoy this for Bill's sake.*

The assistant pastor gave the welcoming remarks and announcements. The congregation sang a song, enjoyed a fellowship moment when everyone shook hands, then remained standing for the offertory hymn. After another exciting number by the choir, the pastor, Dr. Miller, came to the podium to speak, and all eyes turned toward him.

"Before I start my message this morning, I want to depart from procedure a little. As you all know, we came very near to losing one of our beloved members just two weeks ago in a football game. Buck, come up here for just a moment. Can you make it?"

Bill looked genuinely surprised, but he regained his composure, stood, and limped toward the front of the church, leaning on his cane. *He's leaning on it a little too much*, Janice thought. *What kind of act is this? He got around better at home without it.* As he walked down the aisle, a small ripple of applause began around him, then grew, and soon the entire congregation was standing and clapping, many openly weeping. Janice frowned in confusion.

Bill struggled up the two steps to the platform with the help of the choir director, wiping tears from his face as he went. He hadn't expected anything like this. These people loved him as a brother, not because he was famous. He knew it had been their prayers that had brought him back when he had wanted briefly and insanely to die. With a grateful smile, he lifted his hand and waved to his much-loved church family, and the applause crescendoed.

I can't believe his grandstanding, Janice thought. *This is really too much.*

"I just want to say thanks for your prayers," Bill continued. "You're all terrific . . ." He paused, working to regain his composure again. "And let me tell you something . . . Don't you ever let anyone tell you that God's not real because I was . . . I was dying . . ." His voice broke as he spoke. ". . . and I felt the real presence of Jesus."

Janice looked at him in amazement. He'd never told her that. What kind of game was he playing? He had obviously moved the other people, however. Many were saying "Amen," "Praise the Lord," or "Hallelujah."

"I had a reason to come back though," Bill said. "There's a very special lady . . . Janice, raise your hand so everybody can see you."

Janice blushed and pressed her hands to her sides as everyone turned to look at her.

Bill grinned. "She's a little shy. But as you all know, we got married last week. And we have a twelve-year-old son."

"That was fast work," someone said, and the room erupted in laughter.

Bill laughed too. "Seriously, I'm sure most of you know by now, Janice and I were married as kids. We just decided to put our lives back together."

Dr. Miller patted Bill's shoulder, and Bill returned to his seat amid more pleasant comments in the relaxed service. Quiet settled over the auditorium as the pastor began to speak again.

Janice looked at the people around her. Their eyes were fixed on Dr. Miller. Expressions on their faces ranged from rapt attention to worried conviction as he spoke. Janice tried to listen, and a few of his phrases embedded themselves in her mind. Love. Acceptance. Something like that. It vaguely reminded her of what her mother and Kate had talked about. But for the most part Janice was deeply troubled by Bill's behavior.

She had allowed herself to love him again because of his kindness, humility, and genuine concern for Billy and her. Had the football injury and operation changed him, or was he now just showing his true colors? And this church! While she had to admit that a variety of economic levels were accepted as a part of this church family, the ones who seemed to be closest to Bill were the best-dressed, best-looking ones. How genuine was this church, and did she belong here?

Neither Janice nor Bill brought up the church experience that afternoon, though Bill was deep in thought about it. His Christian friends had shown him warmth and love, yet something was missing. Where was the joy he'd felt for over two years just from knowing he was a child of God? Why did his prayers seem to bounce off the ceiling these days? And why did he feel completely inadequate to even bring up the subject of the Lord to Janice and Billy?

Since becoming a Christian, his habit had been to keep a Bible on the bedside stand and read several chapters before going to sleep. Yet it had been weeks since he'd read the Scriptures. And whenever his hand strayed by habit to pick up the book, a feeling of restless irritation held him back. So his bedside Bible became just one more thing for Janice to dust, though he wouldn't have noticed if she hadn't.

But Janice did dust the Bible—and everything else in the condo, every day. Not satisfied to clean just once a week, as soon as breakfast was completed she'd begin to move through the large condominium like a perpetual motion machine. She wanted to prove to Bill that she could keep up with everything, that they didn't need a housekeeper. She watered the many plants and fed the fish in the three aquariums. She swept the patio, vacuumed every room, and waxed the already shiny kitchen floor. As each day passed and she became more exhausted, she was driven on to new heights of perfection by a fear of failure.

Billy needed to be waited on hand and foot since he still couldn't walk on his healing leg. But Bill was another matter. She had forgotten how sloppy he was. He couldn't seem to understand that he should put his dirty clothes in the hamper, so the last chore of her day was to pick them up off the dressing room floor and put his shoes away. And in the morning she had to use two large towels to wipe down the bathroom after his shower and shave. Sometimes she wondered if he was deliberately making more work for her.

Gradually Janice began to fall behind in keeping things up to her own standard. To her horror, some of the beautiful house plants were dying, though she couldn't understand why. But the biggest heartbreak came when she went to feed the fish one morning and found that one aquarium had lost its entire population overnight. The brightly colored blue, orange, and glistening white exotic fish she had loved to watch were floating near the bottom of the tank, their colors tinged a dull gray.

It was too much! She dissolved in tears on the couch across from Billy.

"Mo-o-om . . . Don't do that . . ." he whined. "What's the matter?"

She mumbled unintelligible words at him, but her glance at the aquarium explained it all.

"Mom, what did you do to the fish? They were fine yesterday."

"Nothing! I cleaned all three aquariums yesterday just the same as always. I even added water and chemicals just like I was supposed to, according to the book on the shelf. Look, the other two tanks are just fine." She jumped up from the couch and took a closer look. "Those fish look okay, don't they?"

"Mom, that's a saltwater aquarium. I read the book too. The stuff about saltwater fish is in the back."

"Saltwater! What will I tell Bill?" She glanced toward the hallway door, then back at the fish tank. He'd be coming at any moment. Maybe if she took the dead fish out and put them down the garbage disposal, she could go buy some new ones before he missed them.

"Tell me what?" Bill interrupted her panicked planning.

"Oh, nothing. I just . . ."

"Janice, what did you do to the aquarium?" He walked over to inspect the large tank. "That white one with the black stripes, the Tinker's Butterfly, cost me over three hundred dollars. And this poor little guy, the one that used to be bluish-purple, is a Red Sea half-moon. It goes for a hundred and fifty. The orange ones you can't get for less than . . ."

"Three hundred dollars! You spent three hundred dollars on a fish?"

"And by the way," he said, ignoring her comment, "what's the deal with the house plants? A bunch of them are turning yellow, and the leaves are falling off that little tree on the patio."

"Yeah, I know . . ." Suddenly she was very tired even though the day had just begun. She had the strong urge to go back to bed and stay there.

But Bill was on a roll. Maybe Janice would give up this silly idea of not wanting help if more things like these were brought to her attention.

"Well, never mind," he said in a consoling tone. "We can replace the fish and the plants. Don't feel bad. Why don't you run out to the kitchen and fix us one of your terrific omelettes for breakfast? And by the way, I've been meaning to tell you, this is southern California, and you can get fresh oranges here just about all year long. I really like that fresh-squeezed juice, honey. There's an electric juicer out there somewhere."

Janice stared at him blankly. The loss of the poor little three hundred dollar fish and beautiful houseplants was her fault. How could she just shrug it off and dash out to fix breakfast? But maybe this was a way to make up for her tragic mistakes. She couldn't possibly fail in the kitchen.

"Sure. Breakfast for two coming right up," she responded, relieved that he wasn't angry. She hurried out to the kitchen. What had he said about orange juice? Fresh-squeezed? How fortunate that she had bought plenty of oranges the day before. She squeezed the fruit juice into glasses until her hand ached. When all the oranges were squeezed, she looked in dismay at the two half-filled glasses. With a guilty glance toward the dining room door, she reached into the refrigerator and filled each glass to the brim from the bottle of reconstituted concentrate.

Eight

SUPER BOWL! JANICE THOUGHT she would scream if she ever heard that phrase again. But she did hear it again—and again and again. Throughout the two weeks following the conference championship games, no matter where she went, she was bombarded with Super Bowl mania.

Every snack food was labeled perfect to eat during the Big Game. Proper clothing was a must while watching The Game, said the advertisements. Every airline beckoned people to fly with them to New Orleans for the most exciting trip of the season. Boats and cars were even raffled off because of the Super Bowl. Janice never could understand that last connection.

The Mason household could hardly escape the celebration. Reporters who had failed to be chosen to represent their newspaper or television station searched for sideline human interest stories. One of the biggest, of course, was Buck Mason. Everyone wanted to write or broadcast the news of how he was taking the crushing blow of missing the chance every professional football player lives for.

Bill was known for being cooperative with the media, but even he began to wear thin after the third interviewer in one day asked about his feelings. He'd said all the right things, and he knew he'd sounded properly "disappointed but pulling for the team." But each time he spoke with reporters, there was a deeper gnawing in the pit of his stomach. The closer game day came, the worse he felt. So he rejected the television network's request to include him in their telecast.

The Mavericks had flown to New Orleans on Tuesday to get accustomed to the artificial turf of the Superdome, where they would meet the Dallas Cowboys the following Sunday. Bill desperately wished to be with them, even just to be on the sidelines. But since his surgery had only been three weeks before, Dr. Bennett vetoed the plan, saying the excitement of being there might cause a serious setback. He had to settle for inviting several former teammates over to watch the game with him.

When Super Bowl Sunday arrived, Janice cleaned the apartment and prepared food for the expected company. By noon the four guests had arrived. One was a retired trainer, and the other three were ex-players.

Janice didn't like the looks of any of them. She bit back her protest over the case of beer the men had brought. How could Bill allow such people to drink beer in front of Billy? She'd made sure the soda fountain was filled. Why wasn't that sufficient? Fuming inwardly, she returned to the kitchen to stir the chili she'd prepared for dinner. How nice it would be to curl up with a good book in her bedroom, she thought. But concern for Billy drew her back to the living room.

After two hours of pre-game shows, Janice found it difficult to hide her boredom. Fortunately, eyes were glued to the television, and no one noticed her yawns. Every starting player's record and ability were discussed, along with the history of each team, the game plan of each coach, and every hangnail the players had had that week. There was a one-minute, pre-recorded segment about Bill too, the only bright spot in the program for Janice. It was far beyond her comprehension how people could be so crazy about a game that seemed to specialize in injuring those who played it. Even more beyond her thinking was the fact that Bill not only still loved the game but was so deeply engrossed in it that he didn't hear her ask if he wanted some chili.

"Bill, are you hungry yet?" she repeated, shaking his arm playfully.

"Shh!" he hissed, shaking her hand away. She retreated in wounded silence to the kitchen during the kickoff. From there she could hear the men shouting and calling from time to time as they cheered for their team. Eventually she brought out another tray of potato chips and dip and sat down to see what all the excitement was about.

Dallas had scored two touchdowns in the first quarter of the game, but the Mavericks fought back and came up with a field goal and touchdown with extra point in the second quarter. Bill had the eerie feeling he was watching himself as his protégé Joey Jones executed many plays Bill had helped design. When Bill called out a play to the television, Joey seemed to hear across the miles and know just what to do.

The half-time show had a country and western theme starring two of Janice's favorite singers. But as she settled in to enjoy the music, Bill reached over and squeezed her ribs playfully.

"Hey, babe, where's that chili?" he said. "We're starving."

"Yeah, Mom, how about some of your three-alarm specialty," Billy said.

The other men chorused their approval of the plan.

"Sounds good."

"Bring it on."

"Yessiree."

But Janice was still processing the word *babe*. Bill had never called her that before. Of all the names she'd been called as a waitress in a truck stop, none of them seemed to her as degrading as babe. It reminded her of Paul Bunyan's blue ox. Any man who had dared to call her that could count on cold food and cold coffee.

In icy silence she rose and once again resorted to the kitchen, casting one longing glance at the television. She bit her lip to stifle her disappointment over missing the world champion cloggers who were about to perform.

The men carried on their conversation in loud and boisterous voices, and occasional profanity reached Janice's ears. Why wasn't Bill protecting Billy from these crude men? How could he not know he'd hurt her feelings? Was he drinking beer along with his guests? She peeked out the door and was relieved to see a soda in his hand. Not really interested in the game or the camaraderie, Janice nevertheless sat down in the living room for a few minutes of rest.

Apparently Coach Chuck Speer had done some strong talking to his team during half-time. The Mavericks' energy was high as they burst onto the field for the second half. Bill and his friends made several jokes about Speer's ability to recharge his lagging team, each of them having been on the receiving end of his sharp tongue. But the Cowboys' famous coach had talked to his team, too, and the two teams pushed each other back and forth across the field like two equally matched sumo wrestlers.

The game seemed to drag on forever. Late in the fourth quarter, on fourth down in a Mavericks' drive, with the Cowboys still leading 14-10, there was no time left for caution. At the Cowboys' 30-yard line, the center snapped the ball to Joey, who handed off to running back Keith Peal. Peal headed toward the left end for a sweep as Joey dropped back out of the action.

Knowledgeable fans were disappointed at the choice of plays, figuring the Cowboy defense would easily stop the action. But Peal stopped suddenly and deftly flipped the ball back to Joey, who stood free and clear well behind the line of scrimmage. He caught the ball and quickly fired it to Scott Lansing in the end zone. With a diving catch, Scott reached for the overshot missile and cradled it in his arms. Touchdown! The Cowboy defense pulled back in disappointment. Scott jumped to his feet and danced around, holding the ball over his head triumphantly.

It was the same surprise play Bill had used against the Omaha Aces. Even though Joey had overshot his target, Scott had made it work. Once again the team had worked together to perfection. The extra point made the score 17-14, and when the

Cowboys were unable to score in the last moments of the game, the Mavericks were the new Super Bowl champions!

The living room rang with cheers, high fives, and raucous laughter. The men called for more food and drinks and watched the replays, celebrating well into the evening.

Despite his protests, Janice put Billy to bed, then retreated to the kitchen to clean up the dishes. She could hear Bill laughing and joking with his friends as he walked them to the door. There was a burst of laughter as the men shared one final joke before a welcome silence settled over the apartment.

Janice slowly pushed open the swinging kitchen door and peered out to make sure the guests had all departed. Bill stood beside the dining table flipping a football from one hand to the other, his jaw set in anger, his eyes narrowed. Suddenly, with a snarl on his face, he flung the ball the entire length of the apartment. It sailed through the open patio door, smashing into a small concrete planter on the railing. The planter crashed to the patio below while the ball bounced back crazily, hitting the glass door with a bang and coming to rest next to a lounge chair.

Bill's left hand gripped his abdomen as he bent over slightly. Then in renewed anger he slammed his right fist against the dining room table, causing the glass top to clatter against the ebony frame. Amazingly, it didn't break.

"Well, that's one way to celebrate your team winning their stupid game," Janice said. "Shall I clean up the living room now or wait until you break a few more things?"

He looked at her in angry confusion, as though trying to figure out who she was. As her words sank in, he gave a short, bitter laugh.

"Thanks a lot, Janice. You're really a big help, just when I need you the most." He spun around and limped toward their bedroom, slamming the door behind him.

Rage boiled inside Janice. How dare he invite rude men into their home, treat her like a servant, call her a degrading name, and then have the nerve to be angry with her! He would pay for this day. He would pay dearly!

Janice awakened to Billy's call and nearly fell off the couch as she turned over to respond to it. Disoriented, she clung to the couch back until she could remember where she was. As her memory focused on yesterday's Super Bowl game and her few bitter words with Bill, sadness crept over her. Last night he'd gone to bed without her, and she hadn't entered the bedroom even to get her pajamas. She had dropped onto the couch in anger, pounding the throw pillows with her fists, then throwing some of them at the television. But the vengeful feelings gave way to the depression now filling her heart. For the first time since Billy's surgery, she didn't run to answer his morning call for help to get out of bed.

As angry as she might have been at Bill, she could never plot serious revenge. Self-punishment was more her style. Why had she married Bill again? Why hadn't she recognized that he was still the same self-centered brat he'd always been? It was her own fault she was in this mess.

"Oh, God, what am I going to do?" she whispered. Startled by her own words, she realized that she had just prayed for the first time in days. *Yes*, she thought, *what am I going to do, Lord? How can I get Billy and me out of this mess?*

A gentle peace warmed her heart. God was so good! He always heard her prayers, even when she'd been ignoring Him. She was still depressed, but somehow she knew the Lord would show her what to do.

"Mo-om!" Billy called.

"Coming," Janice called back. Then she wondered if any of their neighbors in this fancy building could hear their Colorado-style communication. "I'll be right there," she yelled just a little louder.

"Mom, how long do you think it will be before I can get this brace off?" Billy asked as Janice helped him into his wheelchair.

"You ask me that every day. You know Dr. Bennett says it's important not to hurry. You haven't been turning those screws too much, have you?"

Billy rolled his eyes. "No, I haven't been turning those screws too much," he said in a mocking voice.

"Billy . . ." Janice said, her heart sinking at his tone.

"I'm okay, Mom. Don't worry about it. I'm doing what the doctor showed me."

She frowned at his impatience with her, but before she could scold him, the bedside telephone rang, and she turned to answer. Bill had picked up their bedroom extension and was talking to Coach Speer. Bill sounded so cheerful. Janice hung up the receiver, her heart doing flip-flops with her stomach. He was good at keeping up a front with his friends. How would he treat *her* this morning?

She helped Billy dress himself as much as he would allow, then wheeled him into the living room, handed him the remote control, and went to the kitchen to fix breakfast. She would act as though nothing had happened. No, she would be very cool to Bill. No, she would fix cold cereal. But that wouldn't do. Billy should have something warm. She returned to the living room to ask her son what he wanted just as Bill entered from the hallway and solved her dilemma.

"That was Speer," he said, his voice filled with excitement. "He and Brooks want me to meet the plane at the airport in a couple of hours. They're sending a limo. He said they want me in the parade downtown this afternoon. And they want me to fly to D. C. Wednesday to meet the President with the team. It's tradition. The winning team always goes to the White House. It's an honor . . ."

"Hey, Buck, that's great," Billy shouted. "See, they just can't do without you!"

Janice held back the tears trying to form in her eyes. She

glanced at her son, then back at Bill, who stared at her with a strange, almost defensive expression. Her mind raced to keep up with the conflicting emotions sweeping through her—hurt over yesterday, sympathy for his disappointment, an unexpected pride that he would meet the President of the United States, bewilderment over Billy's rudeness. At her hesitation, Bill started to turn away.

"Do you want some breakfast before you go?" she asked.

Bill turned back, his eyes revealing hurt. She had chosen the wrong thing to say.

He shook his head. "I'll get something on the way."

Janice stared after him as he returned to their bedroom and closed the door. Her mind struggled to find some way to reach out to him in spite of her own hurt feelings.

"Mom?" Billy said anxiously. "What's going on? Aren't you glad for Buck?"

She could no longer hold back the tears as she turned to her son. "What?"

"Mom, how come you're crying? Aren't you glad he gets to go with the team? Man, I wish I could go with him."

Janice studied her son's eyes for a moment, really seeing him for the first time in days. He looked vulnerable and bewildered, and his confusion was her fault. After all the months she'd spent praying for him to be reconciled with Bill, after all the heartaches of the past ten years, how could she not put her own feelings aside for her son now? She would do whatever it took to make him happy.

"Sure, I'm happy." She tried to smile so her tears wouldn't prove her a liar. "I'm just a little tired, that's all. I'll go help him get ready." She tousled Billy's hair and walked toward the bedroom.

Billy frowned at her back, annoyed. What was going on with her anyway? Didn't she realize how lucky they were to be living with Buck Mason, his very own dad? Didn't she realize how fortunate it was that Buck still wanted them to be a family? Through the years it had been just he and Mom. Billy knew what it was like to be on the outside. He'd had very few friends growing up, and none of them were real buddies. But Buck was popular. He was on the inside. His team couldn't do without him, even when he was on the injured list.

Injured! Billy felt his heart twist inside him. It was his fault Buck was injured. He'd wished Buck was dead, and he'd almost been granted his wish. Now he had to make it up to him. And he had to make sure Mom didn't do anything stupid to mess things up.

Janice stood in the hallway, her hand hesitating on the doorknob. What could she say to cool Bill's anger toward her? She entered the room slowly and watched him dress in his casual slacks and pullover shirt with the Mavericks logo. His clothes were loose from his dramatic weight loss, and the sight was a stinging reminder to Janice of all they'd been through. Why couldn't she keep her mind on what counted? He was still alive, and he belonged to her!

Walking across the room, she cleared her throat. "I didn't vote for him, but I'd still like to meet the President."

Startled, Bill looked up from tying his shoe. He stared for a moment into her eyes as though checking her sincerity, then returned to his task. "Yeah, same here. It's not the man, it's the office. Some people call it the most important position in the world."

"Yeah."

The room seemed to echo with silence, and Bill seemed to fuss with his shoe laces longer than necessary.

"May I help you get ready?" Janice said.

He looked up again and shrugged. "Sure. I'd like that breakfast you offered."

"Eggs okay?"

"Cereal's fine."

"The one with your picture on the box?" She gave him a little smile.

He grimaced. "You know, I really hate that stuff."

Janice exploded in laughter at his unexpected confession. "You hypocrite! Thousands of adolescent boys torment their mothers to buy it, all because of you."

He grinned sheepishly. "I didn't say it isn't good for them. Just that I don't like it."

"I ought to make you eat it." She laughed again and turned to leave.

"Janice?"

She turned back just as Bill strode across the distance separating them and grabbed her in his arms. With a deep sigh, she rested her head against his chest as he held her. Was it he who was trembling or she? When he gently lifted her chin and kissed her, their tears mingled on their lips.

For several moments they absorbed the comfort of each other's arms. Then he whispered, "I have to go soon. Will you be okay?"

She nodded, hiding her disappointment that this moment had to end.

Suddenly energetic, Bill held her at arms' length. "I almost forgot—Saturday night we're having a celebration bash at the Hilton. You have to get a dress, a really special one. And I have to get my tux altered. Can we do that by Saturday?"

Reality smacked her in the face again, but Janice was determined that this time it would not be a problem.

"I'm sure we can." She smiled, but her heart was in her throat. Dress? What kind of dress? All these questions—and Kate wasn't even here to help her.

That afternoon Janice and Billy watched the local sports channel on their big-screen television as Bill and the other

Mavericks paraded through the city and were welcomed by the mayor and governor at City Hall. Billy took it upon himself to give her a running commentary on every happening, instructing her on the respect due to each player for this or that amazing play successfully executed at some time in his career. He was pleased that his mother's attitude had improved but felt the need to keep her straight.

Unaware of her son's concern, Janice nodded as though she understood his football chatter. It always surprised her how he could remember details of past games, but she certainly didn't retain any of the names or information he was dispensing. As she watched the telecast, she began to wonder if some sort of protocol was being observed in the way attention was focused on both Joey Jones and Bill, as well as on Scott—the captain and Most Valuable Player of the Super Bowl game—and Coach Speer. Remembering his barely subdued arrogance at Bill's welcome home party, she found herself resenting Joey's success. She was surprised to also find herself delighted at the attention Bill received.

As the afternoon wore on, however, she began to worry as his face grew more tired. She wished he was home where she could take care of him once again. How could he manage a plane trip across the country and a big party next weekend? Maybe Dr. Bennett would veto these activities. But Janice surprised herself once again by hoping the doctor would allow him to participate in everything the team did to celebrate their Super Bowl victory.

— Nine —

TUESDAY, AFTER BEING FITTED for alterations on his tuxedo, Bill left with the team for Washington, D. C. He had suggested that Janice ask the tailor where to buy her dress, then bade his wife and son good-bye, assured that his wife would do as he said. But Janice had never known anyone quite like the flamboyant tailor and would not have felt comfortable asking him for the time of day.

With Kate still out of town, Janice pondered where to begin. *The mall might be the place*, she thought. After a short taxi ride she found herself searching the directory at the Beverly Center mall.

As she stood before Bullock's Department Store, she felt her heart sink. The appearance of the immaculate, well-groomed, stylish young women standing behind the cosmetic counters near the entrance of the store contrasted too much with her own pullover shirt, jeans, and sneakers. She should have worn a dress and heels. But she hated heels. And dressed like this, she couldn't even ask the saleswomen where to look for an appropriate dress, or even what an appropriate dress would be for the upcoming event. Who would believe that someone with her appearance would be attending the Mavericks' Super Bowl celebration? They'd think she was a crazy person.

Janice fled down the wide mall corridor and out the door. On the perimeter of the larger mall parking lot were several small strip malls with less intimidating shops. Bree's Consignment Boutique seemed nonthreatening, so Janice entered and began searching the used clothing for some ideas. She didn't want to embarrass Bill. What should she wear? *Lord, please help me!*

After a few minutes the saleswoman finished with another customer and approached Janice. "How may I help you?" the smiling woman asked.

"I have to go to a party, a big celebration, and I need something to wear," Janice said. As she spoke, she studied the woman's face. It seemed very familiar. "Excuse me, but have we met?"

The woman laughed pleasantly. "I don't think so. But you may have seen me on television about ten years ago. I had a series, *Operation Tiger*."

"Yes, I remember you. Breanne Spencer. Why . . . ?" Janice bit back her question.

But Breanne kept smiling. "Why am I running a second-hand store? Don't be embarrassed. The answer is quite simple. I'm not in television anymore."

"I'm sorry. I didn't mean to be rude."

"It's a natural question and actually one I love to answer. You see, when my series ended, I couldn't get work because I had been type-cast, and my 'type' was out of style. After a while I became quite despondent. I began to drink heavily and take drugs. When I came to the end of all that and nearly died, an old friend picked me up out of the gutter. He cleaned me up and helped me start my own business."

Janice smiled, remembering her mother's similar experience. "Really? How wonderful."

"Yes, He is wonderful. His name is Jesus Christ."

Tears formed in Janice's eyes. She had fled the mall feeling like a failure, and God had sent her to this obscure little shop and this understanding Christian woman.

"Now what can I do for you?" Breanne asked. "Oh, yes—a party dress for a big celebration. Tell me all about it."

"It's sort of a football party. I mean, well . . . I'm not sure. My husband called it a celebration bash. His team won the Sup . . . They won their game, so there's a big party."

The woman laughed. "Don't be shy. You must be married to one of the Mavericks, right? I thought so. Well, come over here, and let's see what we can find." She led Janice to a rack of formal dresses in surprisingly good condition. Many looked new.

"I still have friends in show business, so I get a lot of things they've worn maybe one time, or maybe not at all. Take a look at this teal satin. It once belonged to Angela Bains."

Janice gasped. "No!"

"Yes, it really did . . . Oh, you mean no, you don't want it. Okay, how about this one?"

She selected a long, soft pink gown. "This would be very appropriate for a Super Bowl ball."

"It's pretty," Janice said, her head still reeling from the sight of her former rival's old dress. The teal satin was a very sexy, low-cut gown. Had Angela Bains worn it for Bill?

"He likes me in pink." *I'll bet that teal really lit up Angela's gorgeous blue eyes.*

"I can see why," the woman said, holding the dress up to Janice. "You have a lovely complexion, and the pink brings out the green in those beautiful hazel eyes."

Janice took the dress to the fitting room and tried it on. The modest scooped neckline revealed the heart pendant she always wore; and though the dress hugged her body, its soft fabric still allowed freedom of movement. She stepped out of the tiny room to look in the three-way mirror.

"It's lovely, dear. Really, it is. It's a close fit, but elegant instead of seductive. It suits you nicely. Some matching heels and, let's see, your hair will have to go up." She stood behind Janice and pulled her long hair into a French twist.

With memories of Angela Bains still painfully fresh, Janice

wilted from her own silent comparison of herself with the actress. "I don't know . . ."

Breanne turned her around and held her at arms' length like a scolding mother. "Now you listen to me, young lady, you have the look of a scared rabbit, but you're a very beautiful woman. I don't know who you're married to, but even if he's a third-string benchwarmer, this is the dress to make your honey proud when you're with all those other football wives. I'm not just trying to make a sale. In fact, you can have this dress for half-price just to prove I mean it."

Janice smiled at the woman's candor. "Okay, I'll take it. Thanks."

She changed her clothes, paid the bill, and browsed through the racks of used jeans while the woman put the dress in a hanging carrier. As she started out the door, her new friend stopped her.

Taking Janice's hand and staring into her eyes, Breanne said, "The Lord didn't bring you here today just for a dress, although I think that's a special blessing He planned just for you. But I also believe He wants me to inform you that no matter how others accept you or how you accept yourself, you are loved and accepted by Him. He loves you apart from anything you do or anything you are—not because *you're* good, but because *He's* good."

Memories of Dr. Miller's sermon echoed in her mind at the woman's words. He had spoken on that very topic, using almost the same words.

"Thanks. I'll try to remember that," she said.

But if God loved her so much, why had He smacked her in the face with Angela Bains in the midst of this blessing?

Despite her trepidation, Janice continued to surprise herself as she planned for the Mavericks' party. She called the hairdresser who had arranged her wedding hairdo and makeup and made an appointment for Saturday. The woman would come to the condo in the early afternoon and perform her magic once again. Janice decided that she would learn all she could about applying makeup so she could do it for herself in the future.

When Bill returned from the White House trip suffering from fatigue, Janice began to wonder if they should forget the celebration. But he assured her that two days of rest would restore his energy.

In the face of his determination to attend, she fed him pasta, steak, potatoes, vegetables covered in cheese sauce, and rich, creamy desserts, trying to restore some of his lost weight. And with nothing to do but rest and play video games with Billy, Bill ate whatever she put in front of him. It pleased her to serve banana splits to her two men as they sat by the Olympic-size swimming pool, soaking up the California sunshine.

On Saturday the tailor returned the tuxedo, and it fit Bill perfectly. Janice looked stunning in her new dress and hairdo. And Billy assured his parents he would call the doorman on duty if he had any problems. A limousine would arrive at the appropriate time, and the attractive newlywed couple could attend the gala football celebration without a worry.

The Beverly Hilton was only the second hotel Janice had ever entered in her life. She had been amazed by the opulence of the Majestic Inn in Denver, where she had stayed when Billy was in the hospital for his surgery. But this hotel was even more elegant. Janice decided that what had been snobbishness in the attitudes of the Majestic staff was sophistication here at the Hilton. But she also couldn't help comparing it to the homey atmosphere of Trucker's Haven where she had waited tables for ten years.

You have to be a somebody to get decent treatment at these places, she thought, remembering a brief but painful snub she had received at the Colorado hotel before the desk clerk knew she was with Buck Mason. But back home at the diner, everybody was just "folks." Everybody was treated the same.

"You okay, sweetheart?" Bill asked. He held her around the waist as they entered the ballroom where the banquet was being held. "You're gonna knock 'em dead, babe," he whispered in her ear.

The pleasant shivers that began to run down her neck at his whisper overrode her feelings of inferiority in their surroundings. But his use of "babe" brought instant discomfort. She turned to give him the long-overdue news that she hated that nickname, but as she opened her mouth to speak, Scott and Kate joined them, and Kate's happy chatter ended their conversation. With a slightly exasperated sigh, Janice relinquished any thoughts of communication for the rest of the evening. After all, she was just along for the ride.

Seated at the head table were Bill and Scott and their wives, Joey Jones and his date—an attractive young actress of growing fame, Coach Speer and his wife, and the two owners of the Mavericks, Ryan Brooks and Rex Beacham, and their wives.

Bill participated in the ceremonies with his usual charisma. No one hearing him accept praise for his contribution to the team's winning season would have dreamed he was stifling pain and rage he himself couldn't define. He wondered if the burning in his chest was from his emotional turmoil or a problem with his physical heart. Only Janice noticed his twitching hand as Joey Jones's acceptance speech went on too long, and she reached out and slipped her hand into his.

Bill glanced at her, and his blue eyes softened as he realized she knew he was hurting. He gave her a tired, grateful smile and squeezed her hand. As he looked into her trusting face, he was suddenly impatient to get beyond all this hoopla and into some sort of meaningful life with his new family.

Team owner Ryan Brooks took the microphone and looked around the room for a moment. There were a few nervous laughs and coughs in the audience; then everyone grew quiet. With a sly grin, Brooks nodded. "That's right. It's time to name the MVP for the year. It's always a tough choice, especially this year. I've been proud of you men. But when it comes right down to it . . ."

Bill felt a surge of anticipation in his chest. This award

would help make up for missing the Super Bowl. He deserved it for all he'd done through the season. A bolt of jealousy flashed through him at the thought that Joey might receive the award. But as quickly as he thought it, he remembered the two years he'd already been named MVP. It was only fair that someone else should get it. Still . . .

Ryan Brooks continued, "This man has set more records and been responsible for more saves than anyone else, plus being a real motivator for the team. So let's hear it for the Los Angeles Mavericks' Most Valuable Player of the Year, Scott Lansing!"

The room erupted in applause as everyone stood to give Scott a much-deserved ovation. Kate's Kansas farm girl whistle could be heard above the crowd as the stunned receiver came slowly to the microphone with a crooked grin on his face. As the applause quieted, he stared at the large trophy Brooks had placed in his hands.

"Man, this is heavy!" he said.

The audience laughed.

"Wow! What do you say at a time like this?"

"How about 'It's about time'?" someone yelled.

Laughter and words of agreement spread throughout the room.

Scott laughed nervously. "This makes it a lot harder . . . I mean . . . Well, first of all, I want to thank Mr. Brooks and Mr. Beacham. And Coach Speer for driving me so hard all these years. And my wife, Kate, and my kids for being so understanding about my crazy career."

There were comments and nods of agreement at every table.

Scott looked out across the team family and frowned. "It just makes it all the harder to do this. I'm . . ." He looked at Kate, who blew him a kiss. "I'm retiring . . ."

Audible groans surged through the room. Only Brooks, Beacham, and Speer seemed unsurprised by Scott's announcement.

"You can't do that—not now," someone called out, and others voiced their agreement.

"I know this comes as a shock, but I've been at this for nine years, and I'm tired of getting knocked down! As some of you know, my father-in-law has been ill for several years. He decided to put his farm up for sale last year, but I talked him into holding out one more season. Well, I've bought the place . . . It's been in Kate's family for over a hundred years, and we want to keep it that way. But I'm not going to be a farmer—we're going to work with troubled teens from Kansas City, Denver, and other major cities and give them a new life."

The room once again erupted in applause.

"And this," Scott said as he held up the check that had accompanied the trophy, "will help get our project started. Mr. Brooks, Mr. Beacham, Coach, on behalf of the Lansing Youth Foundation, thank you from the bottom of my heart!"

Stunned, Bill watched his best friend take his seat. How could Scott have made such a huge decision without even consulting Bill about it? And how could he give up football? As the final speeches were delivered by the owners, Bill stared down the table at Scott and Kate. The two were oblivious to everyone but each other, and the glow on their faces revealed that they were both pleased with Scott's decision.

Bill glanced at Janice. She was watching the Lansings too. When he caught her eye, she gave him an uncertain smile.

"How about that?" she said.

"Yeah," he said with a mild snort, "how about that."

Ten

AFTER CONSULTING WITH FRIENDS who had children in private schools, Bill arranged for Billy to be enrolled in a home tutoring program. Each day while Bill answered some of his many fan letters and Janice cleaned house and created culinary works of art, their son sat at his new computer, communicating by modem with his teachers at Pinehurst Christian Academy. By noon father and son finished their respective duties and parked in front of the television for video games or lay in the sun by the pool sipping lemonade.

Several weeks after the Super Bowl, Bill and Billy visited Dr. Bennett together, an experience that felt like a great adventure to them after being housebound for so long. Better yet, the doctor gave Bill permission to drive on a limited basis.

"You can take the family on short day trips once a week—no more! Billy, I know you're tired of sitting down, but you shouldn't be too active yet. And you, Buck, are absolutely *not* to lift him," she warned.

"Yes, ma'am!" the two responded together, then promptly went shopping for a family car.

After careful thought and much discussion, they chose a luxurious royal blue minivan and had it equipped with a special seat to accommodate Billy's leg. Now the family could see the nearby sights of southern California and make plans to see more as Bill and Billy continued to improve.

As they drove out of smog-covered areas, they viewed beautiful sunsets over the Pacific Ocean, though they couldn't walk on the sandy beaches until Billy's metal brace came off. They took a picnic to the mountains one week and visited Sea World the next. Billy became frustrated with seeing the sights of the world-famous marine park from a wheelchair, so he requested that for the next outing they simply drive past Disneyland.

"I don't want to go in there in that stupid chair," he said. "I want to wait till Buck and I can race each other from one ride to another."

"So where do we go for our adventure for next week?" Bill asked. "What do you think, Janice?"

"I think Billy needs to get his schoolwork done," she said.

"Mo-o-om!" Billy whined. "You're no fun. Besides, I do my schoolwork."

"Well, we'll think of something." Bill smiled to himself. He was certain that Janice was having more fun than she was willing to admit. As soon as he could make longer trips, he'd take her out to the ranch-area housing developments he'd visited last fall. He could hardly wait for the two of them to choose the location for building their own place.

As much as Janice longed for Colorado, she was discovering ways to survive in her new home. She found that by searching the Yellow Pages of the phone book, she could find someone to help her with any problem that came up.

A simple phone call to a plant service brought a consultant who informed her that houseplants in southern California didn't need as much water as those in much drier southern Colorado. The consultant replaced some of the plants that had been damaged by overwatering and cut back some of the others. Within a few weeks, the condominium greenery was flourishing once again.

The saltwater aquarium was a complete loss, but Janice found it easier than she imagined to replace it and the expensive fish. Using her new credit card, she didn't even ask how much it cost.

She remembered sheepishly that she thought Bill had her sign a prenuptial agreement to protect his money when it had actually only been signature forms for a credit card. How could she have known? She'd never even had a bank account. Fortunately she'd never brought it up, so he'd never know how foolish she'd been.

Her favorite pastime was taking a taxi to the nearby shopping center and browsing through the huge grocery store. In time she no longer checked prices but merely bought the ingredients for any new recipe that sounded appetizing. She loaded up on fresh produce, especially a variety of California citrus fruit. Having found the juicer in her well-equipped kitchen, she took great pleasure in serving her family a large pitcher of fresh-squeezed orange juice each morning and icy lemonade each afternoon.

While Bill touted the wonders of his own state, Janice tried to figure out how to lure him to Colorado. With Scott and Kate living less than a hundred miles from her old home, perhaps he would find rural life as appealing as she did now that football seemed to be just a distant memory to him. Only one thing puzzled her. After their one visit to church, talk about God and religion seemed to be distant memories to him as well.

She had forgotten most of the questions she'd wanted to ask him about spiritual things, so to help herself remember, she began to read the well-thumbed but now unused Bible on the bedside table. As she read, she also found herself praying more often. So far God had answered her every prayer, each one a request for something regarding Bill or Billy. Now she often thanked Him for restoring her family. And soon she began to pray for other people who came to mind—her mother, Scott and Kate, her friends back in Colorado, and Hal, a sad-faced doorman who had just begun to work at the condominium.

Each of the uniformed doormen who guarded the front entrance of the exclusive building were polite but formal to the wealthy residents. But since they reminded Janice of the truck drivers she'd served at the diner, it was far more natural for her to be friendly with them than with the other occupants, most of whom she seldom saw anyway. Her chats with the doormen while she waited for a taxi provided useful insights into California living. And their tips on how to avoid being the victim of a crime added to her determination to convince Bill to move.

Janice was particularly drawn to Hal and very much wanted to cheer him up, just as she'd often encouraged despondent truckers back home through pleasant conversation. Hal was a ruggedly handsome man in his mid-fifties who appeared beaten down by life. The deeply-etched frown lines around his eyes looked even deeper through his thick-lensed glasses, and his drooping shoulders and frequent sighs when he thought no one was looking suggested to Janice that he needed some emotional sunshine. So she planned her daily shopping trip when he was on duty.

"Taxi, Mrs. Mason?" The man lifted the phone, anticipating her response.

"No, thanks. I already called." Janice sat in one of the overstuffed chairs near his desk and wondered how to begin.

"It's a nice day to go shopping," Hal said pleasantly.

"Well, nice for California," Janice said. "Tell me something, Hal. Why do people move here? It's so smoggy and overcrowded." As soon as the words were out of her mouth, she regretted them. She couldn't encourage him by complaining!

Hal gave a mild snort and shook his head. "That's a good question, ma'am. I'm afraid I can't help you."

"But why did you come? You weren't born here, were you? You have a little bit of a southern accent."

Hal sighed. "Yes, ma'am. I was born in Georgia. I came out here more years ago than I want to remember." He settled back in his chair and shrugged first one shoulder, then the other in an odd yet fluid movement.

Janice stared at him. A memory, distant but so familiar, teased at the corners of her mind. Where had she seen that gesture before?

"I came out here to be an actor," Hal continued. "Westerns were big back then, and with a slight adjustment to my accent, I thought I'd have it made."

"What happened?" Janice prompted.

"I was in a few movies, as an extra. I took acting and singing lessons, worked real hard at it, but never got past being an extra. I still get a call to do it now and then." He was quiet for a moment, then stared beyond her as though looking down the corridors of his past. "And I had given up everything—family, home, *everything*—to try to be famous. I really thought I had a chance." Hal shook his head and looked down at his hands, almost on the verge of tears. "Now look at me—a failure."

Janice gave him a sympathetic smile, unsure of what she could say that would help. Or should she just say good-bye and leave? Where was that cab? *Help me, Lord.* A thought came to her.

"Hal, did you ever ask God for help?"

The man's head jerked up. "Excuse me, ma'am, I didn't mean to get personal. I think that's your taxi out front."

As Hal held the lobby door for her, she gave him another friendly smile, then walked out to her cab. The peace that filled her heart seemed to assure her she'd been doing what God wanted her to, and she was sure that her opportunity to reach out to Hal was far from over.

The landmark day finally arrived when the doctor told Bill he could begin easy workouts and pronounced Billy in perfect health.

"Well, young man, based on your progress so far, I predict

your left leg will be as long as your right one before the end of April," she said.

"Wow! That's only six weeks away," Billy said. "Hey, Doc, I mean, Doctor Bennett, can I work out with my dad? Just upper body? Sitting down? If I promise to be careful?"

Dr. Bennett laughed. "Billy, you're a chip off the old block, if you'll pardon my cliché. Yes, you're able to do some upper-body exercises now. You really need them since you've basically been sitting down since Thanksgiving. But here's the best news—I want you to begin walking around too. I'll talk to Buck's trainer, and when he comes over next Monday, he'll have an age-appropriate workout for you."

"Cool! Thanks, Dr. Bennett." Billy grinned at the doctor with a boyish expression, then turned to Bill, trying to feign nonchalance over the exciting news. But when he noticed tears of joy in his father's eyes, he glanced down at his hands, cleared his throat, and once again said, "Cool!"

To celebrate their good news, the two drove home from the doctor's office by way of the Burger House, loading up on hamburgers, fries, and shakes and promising each other not to tell Janice.

"She always makes us eat healthy stuff," Billy said, justifying their conspiracy.

"Yeah," Bill said, "we deserve a little junk now and then."

But when they entered the condo, Janice greeted them with a smile that instantly gave way to a wrinkled nose, followed by crossed arms and a scowl.

"You guys smell like . . . Did you think you could keep your little game a secret from me? I can pick up the scent of a hamburger and fries a hundred yards away and three days later," she said.

Her two men exchanged guilty looks.

"Jan, I'm sorry," Bill began.

"Never mind," she said sweetly. "I'll just put away the pizza ingredients I had out for tonight. You know, the yummy, deluxe pizza you both like better than anything else I make? The healthy, low-fat pizza I like to make because it's good for you?"

"Oh, Mom," Billy whined, "give us a break."

"Not at all," she said, turning toward the kitchen with mock wounded dignity. "Oh, by the way, I have some leftover gruel you can have for supper tonight."

They watched her depart through the swinging door.

"Man, we missed out on Mom's delicious pizza!" Billy said, disappointed.

"I can still taste the grease from that burger," Bill sighed.

"Me, too," Billy added sadly.

Father and son exchanged identical grins.

"We'll have to do it again next week," Bill said.

The two laughed as they gave each other a high five.

In addition to answering fan letters, Bill kept in touch with his business manager and his agent. He'd told his agent to refuse any offers for public appearances so he and his renewed family could have time to grow closer. While that was true for the most part, he also felt unequal to the task of delivering either spiritual or motivational speeches. In the two and a half years since he'd become a Christian, he'd spoken at many men's luncheons and youth groups. But the fervency of his faith, which had put all the right words in his mouth on those occasions and had inspired him to search for his ex-wife and son, was no longer part of his life.

When friends called, he turned down social invitations as well, again using the excuse of needing more time to recover from his injury and more private time with his family. Since sports fans were now riveted on the pro basketball season, they left him alone too.

He did manage to offer grace at mealtime, but only because Janice would place the food on the table, then gaze at him with an innocent and trusting look in her lovely hazel eyes. Feeling like a heel, he'd thank God for the food, promising himself to be more of a spiritual leader someday soon, a promise forgotten by the time he said, "Amen."

But now, encouraged by Bill's latest medical report, his agent phoned Bill to urge him to make some personal appearances.

"I've turned down all the out-of-towners," Tom Monroe said, "just like you told me to. But high-school athletic banquets are coming up this spring. You could do one or two locally, or maybe some mall openings or church functions. Oh, we also need to get back to Simmons on your sneakers endorsement, or we might lose it to that new hotshot kid in the NBA. Robert Ruskin called again about that movie for this spring. He's going to begin filming in late April or early May."

For a moment Bill perked up, then sighed with resignation. "Man, I'd love to do that movie, but . . ." He stopped, unwilling to let his agent know that it was Janice's dislike of movie star Robert Ruskin that was holding him back.

"He has a great script. I read it last summer, and I think the part is perfect for you, Buck."

Bill chewed his lip for a few seconds, then said, "Even if I'm back in shape by April, I think I'd better turn it down."

Tom was silent for a moment, then said, "No reason?"

"No reason," Bill said.

The agent sighed in exasperation.

After the call Bill reflected on his decision. He really wanted to do that movie. But it had been too hard to win back his wife and son. He couldn't risk losing them again.

The Mavericks' trainer, Jeremiah Winslow, arrived on the appointed day and was an instant hit with Billy. A man of medium height, he moved with energy that belied his age. Short curly white hair framed his dark face, and deep laugh lines surrounded his intelligent black eyes. When Jeremiah removed his jacket, Billy gasped at the bulging muscles on the man's cocoa-brown arms.

"Wow!" Billy said. "Did you used to play football?"

"No," Jeremiah said, laughing. "But I need arms like these to work over the young guys who do play the game."

"Work us over is right," Bill said. "This guy can cause more pain making me feel good than anyone I know."

Janice was bringing a large hamper of laundry out of the master bedroom as the men walked down the hall toward the room that had been converted into a home workout center. Seeing them, she set the hamper down and smiled. "Oh, I didn't know we had company. Is this your trainer?"

"Yes, sweetheart. This is Jeremiah Winslow. Jeremiah, this is my wife, Janice," Bill said, squeezing her shoulders affectionately.

"How do you do, Mrs. Mason. I'm glad to meet you." The trainer smiled warmly.

"Nice to meet you," Janice said. She reached out her hand, but before it touched Jeremiah's, a gentle swaying of the building made her teeter ever so slightly.

The man leaned forward with a laugh and squeezed her fingertips. "We Californians love those tremors!" he said, winking at Billy.

Billy and Bill joined his good-natured chuckle, but Janice glared at Bill.

"Bill!" she said crossly.

"What?" he said, laughing and shrugging. "What do you want me to do? Every time there's a little tremor, you look at me like it's my fault."

"No, Buck, that's San Andreas's Fault," Billy quipped.

The three men laughed again.

"Pretty sharp boy you have there, Buck," Jeremiah said.

"Very funny," Janice snorted, grasping her hamper and marching toward the kitchen. "Jeremiah, make him suffer for me, will you?" she called over her shoulder.

"Speaking of suffering, let's get with it, Buck. We have a lot of work to do before July training camp rolls around," Jeremiah said.

"Hey, Mr. Winslow, did Dr. Bennett tell you that I get to work out too?" Billy asked.

"That's *Dr.* Winslow," Bill said. "He has a Ph.D. in physical therapy."

"Billy, you can call me Jeremiah. And, yes, Dr. Bennett told me to get you in shape too."

"Double cool! Thanks, Jeremiah."

The routine began slowly. Jeremiah checked the workout machines in Bill's home gym and made notes about ordering some additional equipment. He took Bill's pulse and blood pressure, then put him to work on the moving stairs. He went through the same ritual with Billy and started him on a machine to exercise his arms.

"So, Billy," he said, "how do you like Sunday school?"

Billy glanced at his father, then pushed against the padded weights with a grunt, waiting to answer until the exertion was over. "Uh, I've never been to Sunday school."

It was Jeremiah's turn to look at Bill.

Bill avoided his gaze, however, staring instead at the mirrored wall to check his gait.

The older man nodded. "I thought so," he muttered. Aloud he said, "The Lord was mighty good to your dad, don't you think?"

"Yeah, I guess so," the boy said.

Jeremiah frowned for a moment, then broke into his usual smile. "You tell your dad you want to go to Sunday school. I know he's got that fancy minivan all fixed up so you can ride in style. You need to get out and meet some kids your own age. There are some great kids at your dad's church. And some real pretty girls too." Jeremiah winked at Billy.

Billy wrinkled his nose, but then he grinned. It would be fun to meet some other kids. Whoever they were, they would accept him because he was Buck Mason's son. No more teasing because he was crippled. He'd soon be able to walk as well as anybody. And no more comments on his shabby clothes or the rundown trailer he grew up in. It would be his turn to show off cool clothes and a fancy home. He was a rich kid now.

"That sounds cool." Billy looked over at his father. "So, Buck, when do we go to Sunday school?"

Bill worked the machine with a little more vigor than necessary. *Just when Scott leaves town and quits bugging me about going back to church, this trainer has to come along and butt in.*

"Yeah, we'll have to do that real soon." He glanced at Jeremiah, who stared back, shaking his head sadly. A familiar feeling of guilt surged through Bill, but it was quickly replaced by a quirky sense of reassurance. Since he couldn't bring himself to tell Billy about the Lord, maybe Jeremiah would do it. Shutting off the stair machine, he stepped down and wiped his face with a towel. "Okay, Jeremiah, I think I've worked this machine all I can. What's next?"

The older man pointed to a machine designed to exercise the abdominal muscles. As Bill settled into the seat and reached up for the hand grips, Jeremiah checked the weights.

"Let's start with twelve repetitions."

While Bill counted, Jeremiah checked each movement. Staring at Bill, he said, "I suppose you heard about Hammer."

Bill glanced at the trainer, then back at the ceiling. "Not a word. What's happening?"

"He started drinking again. Not his usual between-seasons, weekend partying either. They say he hasn't been sober since the playoff game when you were injured."

Bill winced. "That's too bad." He grunted with effort to finish the last repetition, then sat back and again wiped the sweat from his face. He started to tell Jeremiah about Jared Hammer's visit to the hospital, but the memory provoked that all-too-familiar pang of guilt. The words of forgiveness he'd spoken to Hammer then would stick in his throat if he said them today.

Jeremiah added, "It's a real shame that he can't understand how much God loves him and wants to be involved in his life. I guess the problem with most people is that they want to be in charge, and they figure if they let God have control of their lives, they won't get their own way. As if they knew better than God what they need . . ."

Bill stood up abruptly, his emotions suddenly as hot as his body. "What's next?" he snapped.

Jeremiah shook his head again. "Just walk around the room a couple of times; then we'll go on to the leg curl. All right, Billy, let's get you on your feet. We'll do a few steps today, but tomorrow I'm bringing in some parallel bars."

Although the workouts were easy, both Bill and Billy felt winded by the end of the session. The older man monitored their cooldowns, then prepared to leave. After parting pleasantries were exchanged, Jeremiah started toward the door, then turned back.

"Buck, I see you're up to your old habits, leaving a half dozen towels all over the floor. Is your mama working here these days?"

Bill glared at him for an instant, then caught Billy's grinning face in the corner of his eye and softened his expression.

Jeremiah winked at the boy but shook his finger at Bill. "Don't you treat that pretty little bride of yours like that, you hear?" Then he laughed and walked out the door.

Bill turned away so Billy couldn't see his face. It was important that these workouts go well. But after just one session, Jeremiah was already getting on his nerves. Was he going to be this pushy every day?

Eleven

AS JANICE WENT SHOPPING and Billy did his schoolwork, Bill filled his mornings with answering fan letters. Of the thousands sent to him each year, he usually saw only a few hundred chosen by the Mavericks' correspondence secretaries. In previous years his off-season schedule had kept him from answering more. This year, with the forced inactivity, he was finding more time to respond to people around the country and around the world who honored him with hero-worship. The letters came from many kinds of fans: teen boys like his own son, men who had longed to play the game in their younger days and were now armchair quarterbacks, and girls with crushes on him. By his request, the team secretaries answered the latter, though they teased him over the phone about how many women had been heartbroken when he remarried his childhood sweetheart.

He was grateful for his stock of formula answers by which he could personalize his response to each person who wrote him. It was especially helpful to have those prepared answers to letters from Christian young people who had read his testimony in their youth magazines. What could he say to them now? Feeling like a hypocrite, he tried to dash off one more letter to a Christian high school athlete facing persecution from teammates because she wanted to pray before games. Throwing his pen down, he put his head in his hands.

"What am I supposed to do now?" His words were partly

prayer and partly a cry of frustration. But the prayer seemed to bounce off the ceiling, doubling the anguish of his heart. He left his bedroom desk and went to watch television in the living room. Before long Billy joined his father, and the two began their daily video game competition as they waited for Janice to return from the market and fix their lunch.

The chiming of the doorbell came at a bad time for Bill. "Aw, come on, Janice, use your key," he said, punching his control pad to outmaneuver Billy's position on the large screen. When the bell sounded again, he threw the controls on the couch in disgust. Walking the length of the large room, he jerked the door open. "Jan, why didn't you use your keys? . . . Rob . . . Rob Ruskin! Hey, man, come on in." He stood back to welcome the unexpected guest and the young boy with him.

"Hey, man, it's good to see you," the actor said, clasping Bill's hand firmly with one hand and slapping him on the shoulder with the other. Then he turned and drew the boy into the room with him. "Buck, this is my son, Eric. He just came to live with me recently."

"Hey, Eric, how are you doing?" Bill said.

The adolescent boy grinned foolishly and shook his hand. "Wow . . . Buck Mason. I can't believe I'm really meeting you. This is so cool."

"Well, I'm pleased to meet you too. Come on in, guys," Bill said as he led them into the living room. "Let me introduce you to *my* son. Billy, this is Robert Ruskin and his son Eric."

Billy's mouth hung open as he struggled to stand to greet the guests. "Robert Ruskin! Buck, I told you you know everybody!"

The actor grinned at Bill. "Great kids, huh! Sit down, Billy. You don't have to treat me like a king or something."

Billy grinned foolishly, his bright blue eyes wide. Then he glanced at Eric, who was obviously sizing him up. Billy sat back on the couch and gave the other boy a nod. "How ya doin'?" he said.

"Okay," Eric answered.

"What brings you here, Rob?"

"Now, Buck," Ruskin said, "you know why I'm here. I want you to do that movie with me."

Bill groaned aloud. "Man, I would love to do it. But I have to get the doctor's okay for everything, and she has me coming back real slow."

"Movie?" Billy said. "You're gonna make a movie? When? Where?"

"Now, Billy . . ."

"Say, Billy, how would you like to go back to Colorado for a visit while your dad and I make a western?" Ruskin inquired.

"A western? Buck, are you gonna do it?" Billy bounced up and down on the couch with excitement.

"Now, Rob, slow down. I said . . ."

"Yes, and I know better. I've talked to Tom Monroe, and he said you already have the doctor's okay."

"Buck, this is too cool! Say you'll do it," Billy pleaded.

Bill shook his head, then handed one of the video control pads to his son. "Billy, why don't you see if you can beat Eric at this game. Mr. Ruskin and I are going to talk in the other room."

Leading his guest to the dining room, Bill pulled out a chair for him, then sat down. "Look, Rob, I honestly would love to do your movie. I haven't told anyone else why I can't do it, but I have to be honest with you. It took me a lot of work to win back my ex-wife, and I'm not going to threaten my relationship with her by doing something she disapproves of."

The actor nodded. "I see. She's not a movie fan? Ah, now I really see. She's not a Robert Ruskin fan."

"What can I say?" Bill wished he wasn't so transparent.

Ruskin looked at him for a moment, then said, "I don't blame her."

Bill stared at him, surprised.

"I mean it. I've made some movies that aren't exactly family entertainment." Ruskin paused, smiling. "All right, I've made some really, uh, shall we say, *controversial* movies."

Bill laughed. "That's putting it mildly."

"Yes, I know." Ruskin echoed his laugh, then grew serious. "But that was before Eric came to live with me."

"Hey, how about that—we're both new fathers with half-grown sons. I guess you know my story," Bill said.

"You bet. And that story is going to be my next project," Ruskin said. "But for now just let me tell you about this one. I think you'll change your mind."

Bill sighed. "Go ahead. Make it harder on both of us when I have to say no again."

Ruskin cleared his throat. "I never thought I'd change my mind about the films I made. I always thought I was making important statements about life and reality—and making great money along the way. As for Eric, he was living with his mother, sometimes back east and sometimes in Europe. He was like a trophy from my first marriage that I kept on a shelf. Every Christmas when I wasn't out of the country, I'd bring him out, dust him off, buy him a few things, and send him back to his mother."

Bill winced. He'd never written to Billy, much less had him come for a visit. He hadn't even known where his son was for ten years.

Misunderstanding his reaction, the actor said, "I see you understand how I felt. Well, last summer the ex announced she was getting married. That was no problem. I've been married twice since her myself." Ruskin cleared his throat again. "I guess that's nothing to be proud of. Anyway, she called and told me the new guy didn't want Eric around."

Ruskin stood and walked around the table, making certain his son couldn't hear their conversation. The two boys were battling fiercely in a video game.

"I grew up in boarding school and swore no kid of mine would have to, so I said he could come on out here. But I wasn't prepared for how I would feel when he came. I felt so . . . so . . . *protective* all of a sudden. I suddenly understood why some people said what they said about my movies. To make a long story short, this new movie is PG. I mean *really* PG. I almost feel like I have to prove the other end of the spectrum now—that good entertainment can be clean *and* make statements about life and reality. That's the way the old films were, the ones I grew up on. Subtle instead of blatant. I think I'm losing you, Buck," Ruskin said, laughing. "Your eyes are glazing over."

Bill quickly focused on his guest. "No, not at all, Rob. You're just making me want to do it all the more. And I'm really flattered that you want me enough to go to all the trouble of coming over like this. None of that 'my people will talk to your people' stuff."

Ruskin ran his hand through his long sandy hair. "That's only half of it, Buck."

Bill looked at him questioningly.

"I've rewritten the script entirely. Did you read the first one?"

"No. I didn't have time during the season. Monroe said it was good though."

"It was okay. It was meant to be a comedy, a spoof. I doubt that you'd like it. It was intended to make fun of some missionary pioneers who settled in Colorado in the 1870s. Well, 'make fun of' is rather mild. 'Make fools of' is more like it."

Bill frowned and shook his head. In spite of his feeling distant from the Lord, he would not participate in ridiculing Christians. "You better count me out, Rob."

"Wait, Buck, hear me out. I was just getting to the good part. When I wanted you to do the movie last fall and you turned me down, I realized I was asking you to be a hypocrite. People see you as a decent person—all right, a Christian—someone who's not afraid to stand up for what he believes, someone who *lives* what he believes. And it would be wrong to ask you to represent that kind of decent person as a fool. Am I making any sense?"

"Go on," Bill said, feeling very much a hypocrite.

"That's when I rewrote the script. I went back and

researched those missionaries. Some of my characters were based on real people, and they were amazing. I want you to play one of those men, Buck. His name was Angus MacGuinness."

"Scottish. Would I have to do an accent?" Excitement replaced the guilty ache in Bill's chest.

"No. He was descended from Scots who settled in Alabama, your home state. You can brush up on that southern drawl, can't you?"

Bill looked at his friend, his eyes bright with enthusiasm. "Can you bring me a copy of the script?"

"It's right outside your front door." Ruskin strode toward the door to retrieve it. "I've put tabs on the pages where your scenes are," he said as he handed Bill the large softbound manuscript.

Bill shook his head but smiled. "I'll read it, but I can't make any promises."

"That's all I ask." Ruskin sat back down beside the dining room table. "Once you read it, you'll be as hooked as I am." He paused, glancing through the doorway into the living room. "So what do you think of this fathering business?"

Bill followed his gaze, his heart warming as he looked at his son making a new friend. Jeremiah had been right. Billy needed friends his own age. But instead of Bill's having to endure going back to church for his son to find a pal, this one had dropped right out of the sky.

Janice gazed down the long grocery store aisle. She had long ago ceased being amazed at the vast variety of pasta and rice available in this shopping heaven. Now it was simply a matter of what to try today. She had not prepared any dishes from India, so perhaps curried rice should be her choice. Just last week she had noticed a recipe on a package of exotic rice. She reached up to the top shelf, wondering what additional ingredients she would need. This store never let her down. They always had any unusual vegetables or spice a recipe might call for.

Just as her fingers touched the package, it seemed to take on a life of its own, moving away a couple of inches. As she tried to comprehend this oddity, she heard the gentle clinking of bottles on the shelf behind her. Down the aisle several women giggled nervously, and one young mother spoke softly to the fussy toddler seated in her shopping cart.

"Never mind, sweetie, it's only a little earthquake."

"*Little* earthquake?" Janice said to herself. How could anyone call these unnerving earth movements *little?* That settled it! She couldn't stay in this place. Recalling newscasts on the devastating quake just a few years before confirmed her resolve. But remembering Bill's offhand attitude about this geological phenomenon, Janice wilted. He'd never leave. He kept on talking about buying property and building a home for her and Billy in one of the very worst areas. When she voiced her concern, he laughed and told her that when Los Angeles slipped into the ocean, they'd have beach-front property for their ranch. His stale joke and maddening attitude didn't help reassure her a bit.

Glancing down the aisle at the young mothers who went back to their shopping as though nothing had happened, Janice sighed. *Lord, why aren't they scared like I am? Please get us out of this place. Please make Bill want to move to Colorado.* Gentle peace filled her heart as she prayed, and once again she knew that somehow God would take care of everything. He'd answered her every prayer; surely He could change Bill's mind.

But another thought crossed her mind, one that had come to her often in the last few weeks. Bill didn't seem to want to pray as he had before they were married. He didn't talk about the Lord to Billy and seemed to feel uncomfortable whenever she brought up the subject. Wasn't it important for Billy to be saved? Or was he too young? Janice longed for the days when she'd been able to ask Kate questions about the Bible. And before that, there had been Alice back home in Colorado. Both women had been Christians for a long time and could answer her inquiries.

One more thing, Lord, she prayed silently, *I don't understand why Bill won't read his Bible, and I wish he would teach Billy about You. Billy's not listening to me these days, You know. So if it's not asking too much, please change Bill's mind about that as well as living in Colorado. Please make him want to pray and talk about You again.*

With that simple prayer, she again left her problems in God's hands and proceeded to the checkout counter.

Using his control pad, Billy skillfully maneuvered his man through the minefield on the screen. But Eric was no novice at this game, and his man stood ready to ambush Billy's.

"Bam! Gotcha!" Eric cried. "My game!"

"Man!" Billy said, slapping a throw pillow in frustration. Then he smiled. "Good game, Eric. Want to go for two out of three?"

"What else have you got? I'm tired of this one."

Billy pulled the box of video games off the table beside him and flipped through it. He wanted to really impress Eric. But Eric had already beaten him at his best game.

"So, like, what happened to your leg, man?" Eric asked. "I mean, that's a totally cool structure you've got on it."

"Aw, I just broke it when I was a kid," Billy said. "When it was in the cast, it didn't grow as much as my right one, so they had to cut the bone and stretch it out."

Eric looked a little queasy, but he forced a laugh. "Totally cool, man. Is it heavy? I mean, can you walk?"

"Naw, it's not very heavy. I just started walking on it a few weeks ago. My dad's trainer, the Mavericks' trainer—Jeremiah Winslow—is my trainer too, and he's working me out every day." He glanced at Eric to see if that information had impressed him and to see how he was coping with the sight of the metal rods in Billy's leg. He didn't want to gross his new friend out, but he couldn't resist pushing things to the limit either. "About four or five times a day I have to turn these screws here." He grasped one of the screws and turned it slightly. "It's easy. The doctor said the cast should come off pretty soon. My left leg is almost as long as my right one already."

Eric refused to be grossed out, merely nodding with interest as Billy turned the screws. "So does it, like, hurt?"

Billy shrugged. "Not bad."

"Cool. So what have you got there?" Eric said, pointing at the box of video games.

Billy pushed the box toward him. "You choose." He watched while Eric looked through the games, hoping he'd select one that Billy could at least make a good showing in. "Have you ever been in one of your dad's movies?"

"I was in a crowd scene once. It was at a race track, and I was this little kid with an ice cream cone. My dad was being chased, and he had to knock the ice cream out of my hand. They had to shoot it three times, and I kept bawling every time because I sure wanted that ice cream. Here, let's try this one." He handed Billy a cartridge.

Billy laughed. "Did they ever let you have it?"

"Finally. But I was so mad, I threw it down. After that, Dad decided not to have me in his pictures anymore. But I didn't care. I just wanted to be with him. So he'd have me come visit between pictures, mostly at Christmas. It was hard, you know?"

Billy nodded. "Yeah, I know." A familiar hollow ache gnawed at his chest as he remembered the years of believing his father was dead. Then Buck, his hero, the greatest football player in the world, came into his life—and he turned out to be Billy's very own dad. Billy shook his head slightly. He couldn't think about that now. He didn't want to remember the anger, the *hate*, he'd felt for Buck for not being there all Billy's life. Because then he also had to remember that it was his fault Buck got hurt. He'd wished his father was dead and had almost received his wish. Billy shook his head again.

"Yeah, this one's good," he said, handing the cartridge back to Eric. "Put it in, and let's see how bad I can beat you."

Janice gazed through the cab's window at the towering palms that lined Rosa Linda del Sol Parkway. Would she miss these majestic trees when they moved back to Colorado? Would she miss these taxi rides to the supermarket? Probably not, though she had to admit there would be feelings of nostalgia toward the city where she and Bill had remarried. As the taxi stopped in front of her building, she pushed down her feelings of excitement. God had answered all her prayers so far, but how on earth would He change Bill's mind?

Hal greeted her with his usual weary but friendly smile. "How was shopping, Mrs. Mason? What concoction are you going to whip up tonight?"

"I'm going for something really different this time, Hal. Curried rice. Ever tried it?"

"Yes, ma'am. Can't say as I like it much. I like to stick to things like ham with red-eye gravy, biscuits, grits, and turnip greens. Simple stuff."

"How about that! That's what I grew up on too. Good southern cooking."

"Can't beat it," the man said as he held the elevator door for her. "Have a nice day, ma'am."

"Thanks, Hal." Janice smiled at him. She wished he wouldn't call her "ma'am." He was old enough to be her father, and the formal greeting seemed out of place. But that's what money had done for her—it took a waitress from a country diner and gave her instant respect. After all those years of serving truckers, a few of whom were far less than respectful, she wondered if she'd ever get used to her new role.

"Janice, you're back early!" Bill stood as she entered the apartment, then laid something on the chair beside the dining room table. Through the glass top she could see that it was a large book of some sort.

"Honey, this is Robert Ruskin." Bill's face wore a strained smile.

"Janice, I'm glad to meet you. It's obvious why Buck was willing to go to the ends of the earth to win you back," Ruskin said. He rose, walked around the table, and took her two grocery bags. "Where do you want these?"

Janice glared at Bill. What was this man doing in their home?

"Here, Rob, let me put them in the kitchen." Bill grew warm with embarrassment. His guest had better manners than he did.

"Please allow me." Ruskin gave Bill a knowing glance, then walked through the swinging door to the kitchen.

Janice crossed her arms. "Do you have something to tell me?"

Feeling like a naughty boy called into the school principal's office, Bill cleared his throat. "Well, you remember that movie I was offered?"

She nodded. "The one you turned down because of who was making it?" She lowered her voice and glanced toward the kitchen door.

"Yeah, that's the one. Well, sort of. This is different—better. Not that I really knew what the first one was about, but this one . . . Rob said he cleaned it up, so I'm sure it's better." Bill lifted the heavy manuscript from the chair and held it out to her.

Janice looked at the floor, and her arms fell to her sides. With a sigh she started toward her bedroom. She didn't even want to be in the same room as the famous, no, *notorious* actor.

"Well, Janice," Ruskin said, returning from the kitchen, "are you excited about going back to Colorado while Bill makes this movie?"

Janice spun around to face the two men. *Colorado?* Trying

hard to keep her soaring emotions under control, she gave Bill a sweet smile. "I can hardly wait. Bill, honey, can I fix you men some sandwiches?"

Bill grinned foolishly, and Janice had to bite her lower lip to keep from giggling both at him and at this amazing situation. The movie had to be all right, she reasoned, or God would not have so clearly answered her prayer.

"Sure, that's great," Bill said. "Sandwiches would be great. Rob?"

"Well . . ." Ruskin looked into the living room where the boys were now deep in conversation, and a gentle expression came over his face. "Thanks. Sandwiches would be fine."

Twelve

JANICE TOUCHED THE POCKET of her new pink suede jacket. Yes, the small package of Dramamine was still there just in case she had motion sickness. Bill had promised that this huge airplane wouldn't bump around like the tiny jet in which she and Billy had flown to Los Angeles four months ago. But it wasn't motion sickness that concerned her—it was the idea of flying at all. Why couldn't Bill have agreed to a nice, slow drive from California to Colorado?

Janice fussed with her seat belt, making sure it was tight, then glanced toward the window for a good-riddance look toward Los Angeles. It had been very easy for her to agree to Bill's calling Mrs. Brown back to take care of the condominium. With luck, no, with *prayer*, they wouldn't be coming back.

In the seat beside her, Billy pressed his face against the window to watch the ground crew make final preparations for the flight. Unconsciously, he reached down to support his left leg's brace as he pushed himself up for a better view. But the metal frame was no longer there. He plopped down in his seat and extended both legs in front of him. They were still the same length, just as they had been when Dr. Bennett had taken off the device he'd worn since last November. He wiggled his legs, unaware of the blissful grin on his face. But adolescent self-consciousness kicked in, and he glanced at his mother, then grimaced and shrugged. She had that expression on her face, the one that made him squirm, like she was either going to kiss him or scold him for something or other.

"I know, I know, my seat belt," he said, buckling himself in tightly.

Bill looked across the aisle at his family, wishing he could be seated beside Janice to take her mind off of flying. But Billy had begged for a window seat, and Janice insisted on sitting beside their son. Bill was grateful that some pre-flight anxiety had been avoided when the airline allowed them to wait in a private lounge until the rest of the passengers had boarded. With dozens of people walking past them in the first class section, someone would surely have recognized him, even with the beard he'd grown for the movie. And that would have slowed the entire boarding operation if someone asked for his autograph or felt obligated to tell him how awful it was that he'd been injured. The autographs made Janice uncomfortable, and the sympathy was more than he could cope with these days. Why was there so much speculation that he would never play football again? And why so many rumors that Joey Jones would soon be given a new contract as the Mavericks' first-string quarterback?

Bill fussed unnecessarily with the air conditioning vent above him, then dug into his carry-on bag for his script. He wanted to be sure he had all his lines memorized. But as he opened the large book, the plane began to taxi toward the runway, and he heard Janice gasp softly. Reaching across the aisle, he grasped her hand and smiled.

"Colorado, here we come," he said.

She smiled at him weakly, only a little encouraged. *Lord, help us. Please help us*, she prayed repeatedly as the mighty jumbo jet roared down the runway and soared into the early-morning sky.

Swept along by brisk April winds, clouds of powdery snow flew down from the mountain peaks west of Highway 25 and glistened in the bright Colorado sunshine. Beneath the white carpet that still covered the Sangre de Cristo range lay the deep padding of a long winter's icy deposits. But on the eastern plains, the vernal season had tossed countless green throw rugs on the brown prairie grass. Only in the shadowy northern sides of the rocks and hillocks could dusty patches of snow elude spring's sunny, windy broom.

Despite the warm interior of the stretch limousine, Janice shivered. She had forgotten how cold Colorado could be. Her waist-length suede jacket had been more than she needed as they left Los Angeles, but at the Denver International Airport the Colorado wind had cut through her jacket and jeans like a knife. For a moment she wished she'd brought her full-length mink coat but was immediately glad she hadn't brought it. How could she wear such an ostentatious wrap in front of Mac and Gracie? It was bad enough to be arriving in this fancy car the movie studio had insisted they use.

"Excited?" Bill asked, giving her a squeeze. "Hey, you're shivering. Are you cold?"

"Oh, no," Janice said. "Not really. Well, not too much."

Bill tweaked her nose. "You're freezing and you know it! Did you forget what springtime's like in the Rockies? The old 'windchill factor'?"

She lifted her chin and gave him an impish grin. "I'll take windchill over earthquakes and smog any day."

Bill laughed. "You're cute when you're stubborn." He gave her a quick kiss, then another more lingering one. "I'll warm you up, my little icicle."

"Yuck!" Billy snorted in disgust. "Do you guys mind?"

Bill and Janice laughed as their son squirmed in his seat.

"Just you wait," Bill told him. "You'll discover girls someday."

Janice resisted the urge to reach over and tousle Billy's hair. "Honey, are you as excited about seeing Mac and Gracie as I am?"

Billy's eyes lit up. "Yeah. I can't wait for them to see . . ." He looked down at his legs, then stretched them out, once more making sure that they really were the same length. An annoying lump came to his throat, and his eyes started to sting. He glanced at his parents, who both had that goofy expression on their faces. Were they going to cry about his leg again?

"I can't wait to see if they got all my important stuff out of the trailer," he said quickly.

Janice cleared her throat. "Honey, I've told you a hundred times, Frankie and Alice got all your posters and rocks and stuffed toys . . ."

Billy glanced at his father. "Yeah, well, I don't need any stuffed toys. As long as they got my football and my wood-carving kit, they can give those stupid stuffed toys to their kid."

"Even Binky?" Janice teased.

"Mo-om!" Billy whined. He jammed his hands in his pockets, hunched his shoulders, and stared out the window, doubly annoyed when his parents laughed at his complaint.

Janice snuggled closer to Bill, savoring the warmth of his embrace. Through the dark tinted windows of the limousine, she gazed at her beloved Colorado landscape. She was certain God had brought them back to her old home for good. Somehow Bill would see what a clean, peaceful place this was and would want to stay.

Each day when she read her Bible, she found verses that seemed to promise God would give her whatever she asked for. True, several small things had not gone quite her way recently. In fact, it had been a big disappointment that Eric Ruskin would be on the movie set and Billy was planning to spend all his time with him. She was concerned about that boy's influence on her son. But her prayers that Scott and Kate Lansing would drive over from their Kansas farm to spend a few days with the Masons had received an affirmative answer. And the best answer of all was, she and Billy and Bill were a family again—*a family in Colorado.*

The limousine passed through Pueblo and continued south

on Highway 25. Janice and Billy watched in anticipation as they passed familiar landmarks. In the distance the tops of several eighteen-wheeler trucks could be seen parked on the right side of the road. As they passed over a small rise, the picture became complete: Trucker's Haven Diner, the nearby motel, and the trailer court where Janice and Billy had lived for ten years before Bill had reentered their lives.

"Is that the place, sir?" the limousine driver asked over the intercom.

"That's the place," Bill said, his tone not betraying the flurry of emotions vying for control. Janice was delighted to be back here, but the place had few fond memories for him. Would he ever be able to forget the horror of finding out what a dump Janice and Billy had lived in for so long? Would the feelings of guilt over his neglect ever disappear?

Billy knelt by the door of the limousine and pressed his face to the window, gripping the door handle so he could spring out as soon as they stopped. Despite his earlier plans to play up arriving at the diner in the luxurious chauffeured car, all he could think of now was seeing Mac and Gracie Devine, his "adopted" grandparents. They were the ones who'd been there all his life when he and his mom needed anything. What would they ever have done without Mac and Gracie? He cleared away the annoying frog in his throat that seemed to jump up every time he thought of the couple. He couldn't wait to show them his leg!

The long black car pulled into the gravel parking area in front of the diner, looking more than a little out of place as it awkwardly moved past several semi-trucks. Momentarily unsure where to park his vehicle, the experienced driver finally pulled up near the front door just as Mac and Gracie Devine bustled outside, arms outstretched. Behind them came their son Frankie, his wife Alice holding the grandbaby, and a couple of Janice's truck-driving friends.

"Billy, honey, come here, boy!" shouted Gracie.

Billy lunged out of the car and into her arms, hugging her

ample form with enthusiasm. He pulled free from her arms and sprang into Mac's embrace, slapping the old man on the back.

"Just look at you," Gracie said, wiping the tears from her face with her apron. "You've grown a foot taller since last December. And look at your leg, as long as the other!"

"Janice!" Mac embraced his former waitress and planted a fatherly kiss on her cheek. "I finally get to kiss the bride!"

"Oh, honey," Gracie said to Janice, "you look so healthy! Just look at that glow on your face. A little color from that California sunshine? And you finally put on some weight and don't look like a poor little waif no more. And who's this?" Gracie glanced past Janice at Bill, who stood by the limousine watching his wife's happy reunion with pleasure.

"Get over here, boy," Gracie said, marching over to Bill before he could move. She reached up and gave him a bear hug. "Are you taking care of my girl?"

"I'm trying to," Bill said with a laugh. He hugged her, then reached out to shake hands with Mac and Frankie. "It's good to see all of you." He looked beyond the Devine family at two men who stood in the diner doorway, one short and wiry and the other tall and rugged. He was somewhat startled by the stern, staring expression on the face of the taller man. It was like looking into the face of an opposing team linebacker. Bill nodded at him pleasantly, trying to ignore the odd feeling that he was being challenged. Who was this guy?

Janice said, "Bill, I want you to meet everyone . . ."

Bill greeted everyone, then shook Frankie's hand a second time. "Thanks for the way you helped Billy out after his surgery," Bill said.

Frankie grinned, trying to relax in the presence of the famous athlete. "Glad to do it. You've got a great kid there."

Janice reached out for the toddler, and he gleefully snuggled into her arms. "He remembers me!"

"Well, sure he does. We talk about you all the time," Alice said, grateful to relinquish the weight of her child for a few minutes. "Oh, Buck, I'm so happy for you all. Janice is such a sweetheart, and I knew when I met her that you two would get back together. It's so romantic!"

"That's George," Janice said, nodding toward the short man who stood by the door. "George is the one who drove me to Denver that night . . ." Janice stopped, wanting to remember George's kindness without remembering that it was Billy's terrifying disappearance that had made the trip necessary. Never again did she want to experience such fear.

"George, I owe you a lot." Bill shook the older man's hand and nodded with approval at the strength in his grip.

"'Tweren't nothin'. I was goin' that way anyhow." George shrugged and grinned shyly.

"And this is Terrell Martin," Janice said, suddenly uncomfortable and trying not to show it. What should she say about Terrell? He had made her realize she was in love with Bill, even as he was confessing his own love for her. Why had Terrell hung around today? He'd normally have his rig on the road to Albuquerque by now. "Terrell's an old friend."

"Martin." Bill nodded as he shook the man's hand.

"Mason." Terrell nodded back, staring into Bill's eyes and holding his hand in a vise grip much longer than necessary. "You take care of her, you hear? There's a passel of us truckers around here who make Jared Hammer look like a wimp, and we won't take kindly to anything going wrong for this little gal." He glanced at Janice, nodded again, and said, "Be seein' you, Janice." He released Bill's hand, slapped on his cowboy hat, and headed across the parking lot toward his eighteen-wheeler.

The group in front of the diner stood in stunned silence for a moment. The reference to Jared Hammer spoke volumes more than the rest of Martin's threat. Janice seethed with anger over her old friend's bad manners. Billy cringed with guilt when he recalled how he'd wished for Buck to get hurt. Bill was filled with a riot of unfamiliar emotions—anger over this unexpected and very public challenge, jealous protectiveness toward Janice, and a terrible sense of his own vulnerability.

A brisk, icy breeze swept through them all, even those used to the windchill.

"Let's go in," Mac said. "We got hot coffee, hot chocolate, you name it. Janice, I hope you all planned to eat a bite with us. Frankie fixed his barbecue ribs."

Shivering violently, Janice stayed close to Bill as they entered the diner. "G-great. I want Bill to taste his wonderful cooking. L-like f-father, like s-son."

"Now don't tell me you've gotten sissified," Gracie teased. "A little chilly wind and you're shaking like prairie grass." She turned and called to the uniformed limousine driver. "Come on in, honey. You gotta eat too."

The early afternoon was a slow time for the diner, so everyone could sit around tables and talk. Time passed pleasantly, and soon both the nippy weather and Terrell Martin's chilling words were forgotten in the warmth of good food and good fellowship.

"Alice, what have you got hiding under that baggy sweatshirt?" Janice asked.

"Well, we figured it's about time this little tiger had a baby brother or sister," Alice said, snuggling her sleeping son close. "This here will be a Thanksgiving baby. We don't know whether it's a girl or a boy, but we want to be surprised, so we're not gonna let the doctor tell us."

"We're thinking we ought to get into a bigger place than our two-bedroom trailer before then," Frankie added. "Business has been improving a little, so I think we can do it."

Janice looked at Bill and smiled coyly. What fun it would be to have another baby! But Bill misread her expression. The wink he gave her had another meaning.

"Speaking of business," he said, "I've been looking forward to seeing all of you in person so we could discuss something close to Janice's and my heart. There will never be any way I can repay you for all you did for Janice and Billy while I was ... Well, while I was living like a self-centered fool. But I do want to try."

"Ain't no need, Buck," Mac said. "She's always been like the daughter we never had. And even though we have our little Alice now, Janice and Billy will always be part of our family. And you, too, of course. Like I always say ..."

"Shut up and let the man talk, Pa." Gracie slapped Mac's arm. "Go on, Buck."

Bill suppressed a grin. These people were like characters in a movie.

"Janice had an idea," he said. "She thinks you can expand your business and still keep it homey for the regulars. Now that I've had some of your great food, I believe in your restaurant as much as she does. I'd like to invest in a new building for you, maybe even see if the motel down the way is up for sale. Combining the two businesses and maybe adding a few other features can turn this into a convenient place for tourists to stop on their way to ski resorts in winter and camping, hiking, and fishing spots in the summer."

For once Mac, Frankie, and Alice were silent, overcome with the prospect of receiving some much needed and very unexpected financial help. But Gracie slapped her knee.

"Praise God! That's just what I've been prayin' for. Thank You, Lord!"

The entire group turned to her in surprise.

"Ma!" said Frankie, "I've never heard you say anything like that."

"Well, I know. But there's some things just gotta be said. You been naggin' me to believe all that stuff about Jesus Christ dying on the cross and I needed to be saved, so I started prayin' that if we got some help with the money around here ... you know you ain't got no insurance, and that baby's got to be paid for ... that I would believe. Well, here's my answered prayer, so I guess I'll just take Jesus up on His offer. I'm gonna be a Christian."

"Well, Ma," Mac said softly, "bless your heart. I never

thought of it that way. But I sure did wonder how on earth we was gonna get out of this mess."

"Oh, Ma!" Alice cried, jumping up and running around the table, baby in arms, to hug her mother-in-law. "Ma, I'm so happy for you!"

Frankie, sitting next to his mother, put his arms around both her and Alice. "Thank You, Lord, for answered prayer." Then he sat back and frowned with concern. "You want to make it official?"

"What do you mean?" Gracie asked.

"Well, I don't want to get legalistic or stuffy about it, but would you like to pray right now?"

Gracie glanced around the group self-consciously. But the loving expression on each face put her at ease. "Yeah, I'd like to do that."

"Okay," Frankie said, "just pray . . ."

"Hush up, boy. You done told me enough times . . . I can do it." Gracie bowed her head, closed her eyes, and held her son's hand. "Now, God, I've called out Your name a lot of times . . . mostly in the wrong way, of course . . . but I can see that You really do care about what happens in our lives down here in this desolate little place on Highway 25 in Colorado, U. S. A. I know Your Son Jesus died on the cross to pay for my sins, and I want to take that free gift of salvation Frankie is always talking about. I want to be saved."

She paused and glanced at Mac, then bowed her head again. "But You'd better save Pa too, Lord, or we're gonna have some rough times around here. And, Lord . . ." She paused again. "Thank You for answered prayer. Amen."

The room was silent for a moment as each person considered what had just transpired. Gracie's face radiated peace and joy, and the deeply-etched wrinkles around her eyes softened. Mac rubbed his chin thoughtfully. Frankie and Alice embraced, squeezing their fussing son between them.

Billy toyed with the salt and pepper shakers, trying to ignore the whole thing. Why did Mac and Gracie need to be saved? They were good people, just like his mom. Not at all like him. The only thing close to praying that he could ever remember doing was wishing Hammer would pound Buck into the ground, and that's exactly what happened. He was a kid who'd wished his own father dead! He would never ever ask God for anything again.

Janice wiped tears from her eyes. Maybe if they stayed here, Frankie could encourage Bill so he'd start talking about the Lord again. And maybe while Bill was making his movie, she could spend her time with Alice, learning more about the Bible and how to help Bill. Surely he'd be too busy filming to need her during the day. Oh, how she missed this homey little diner and, strange as it seemed, waiting on her truck-driving friends.

Bill shifted uncomfortably in his chair, his emotions once again in turmoil. He had started this conversation as a grateful benefactor, but the focus had quickly shifted from his benevolence to Gracie's salvation. It wasn't that he minded not being the center of attention or that his earthly gift had taken a backseat to an eternal matter. What bothered him was his own loss of spiritual vitality. He wasn't leading his family. His infrequent prayers bounced off the ceiling. And he would never be able to portray his movie character without feeling like a hypocrite.

He glanced at Janice and, further irritated by the sweet, trusting expression on her face, was suddenly impatient to be out of this tiny, dingy place.

Thirteen

BILL PARTIALLY CLOSED the large script, stared across the room, and repeated his lines. Today he would face his greatest acting challenge yet. Portraying an actual historical person was a heavy responsibility, even though most people had never heard of the obscure missionary Angus MacGuinness. He found the difference between serious movie acting and the simple, mostly humorous lines in a hair product or sneaker commercial a bit intimidating!

For the past several weeks they had filmed long shots of the wagon train and numerous action scenes involving the entire cast. Thanks to Robert Ruskin's efficient directing and cooperative weather, they had nearly enough of the movie on film to finish it on a sound stage back in Hollywood if the Colorado weather turned bad.

This area of the rugged Sangre de Cristo mountains was both breathtaking in its beauty and breath-giving in the purity of its air. After a week of becoming acclimatized to the altitude, Bill had begun to feel a healthy difference in his lungs. Between scenes, he enjoyed visiting the owners of the ranch where the filming was being done and could envision himself finding happiness in this remote part of the world. But he resisted telling Janice about this. There was more to consider than just liking the clean air and simple life. Billy's education couldn't all be done by computer, and Bill would never consider leaving Janice and Billy here during football season. Besides, there were plenty of clean, quiet places in southern California too.

Bill shook his head and tried again to concentrate on his lines. But memories of his most recent phone conversation with his agent, Tom Monroe, were nagging at him. Ryan Brooks was a personal friend, but he was also a businessman. Joey Jones's incredible performance at the Super Bowl had diminished Bill's bargaining power for his annual contract renewal. Although Dr. Bennett had given him a clean bill of health and had modified her earlier concerns about his heart, Bill was no longer the indispensable king of the hill to the Los Angeles Mavericks.

"Ready for your scene, Mr. Mason." Bill's personal assistant knocked on the door of Bill's luxurious trailer, then opened the door and entered. "Is there anything I can do for you?" the young man asked.

"Thanks, Jason. Yeah, you can bring my script along. Is my makeup still okay?"

"I'm not sure. I think they'll have to add some fake snow to your beard, the kind that sticks. They'll check you before they shoot."

"Makeup sure itches. How can women stand it all day every day?"

"Beats me," the assistant said as he followed Bill out the door.

A cold morning breeze whipped up the powdery snow as it blew through the valley west of La Veta Pass where the film was being shot. The location was several miles from the original Russell, Colorado, which was now a true ghost town with only a few crumbled piles of boards where a booming railroad town once had been. The authentic spot was too near the well-traveled highway to facilitate a convenient movie set, so Robert Ruskin had arranged with the owners of a vast nearby ranch, Rancho Grande de Montoya, to use a corner of their property that had natural features similar to Russell's.

Pulling his coat around him, Bill strode across the makeshift living area where a dozen large trailers like his had been set up to accommodate the film crew and actors. A mixture of excitement and nervousness surged through his chest as he neared the set—a circle of Conestoga wagons set against the real-life backdrop of the snow-covered Colorado Rockies. Could he harness those feelings and use them for his character's motivation? Rob had told him that was the secret to successful acting.

"Bad news, Buck," Ruskin said as Bill approached him. "That jerk Milo has done it again. I told him if he came to work drunk one more time and messed up another scene, he was off the picture. I just got rid of him five minutes ago. We're going to have to get in somebody new, somebody who's built enough like him so we don't have to reshoot all the long shots."

Bill heaved an explosive sigh. "Shoot! I'm not sure whether I'm glad or mad. Here I was all pumped for the scene . . ."

"Yeah, well, it's probably better to call it off," Ruskin said. "You seem a little stressed. You need to relax, buddy. Tell you what, let's take off for a few hours. While casting works on getting us a new wagonmaster, the stunt crew can do some of tomorrow's shots this afternoon. Let's drive into Walsenburg for lunch and take a break from this scene."

"Or better still, we can drive on up and see Janice and the boys. It's been two days."

Ruskin grimaced. "Man, I'm really blowing this father thing. I've hardly noticed that Eric isn't around."

"Don't beat up on yourself. Eric and Billy are probably having so much fun on those new trail bikes, they don't miss us at all."

Ruskin shook his head. "I hope so. Tell you what, let's bring the boys down here for a few days. They're old enough to stay out of trouble."

"Sounds good to me."

Janice glanced out the front window of the diner for the third time in five minutes. It was nearly lunchtime, and Billy and

Eric still hadn't returned from riding their trail bikes in the foothills behind the trailer court. She shouldn't have agreed to Billy's having that stupid motorized bike anyway. Why risk an injury, or worse, so soon after his brace had come off?

Of course, Bill had been all for it when the two boys had come up with the idea. Since both boys had completed the seventh grade early so they could come with their fathers to the movie location, they needed *something* to keep them occupied. Janice was a more-than-willing "baby-sitter" for Eric Ruskin since he kept Billy company. But she would have been much happier if her son could've just gone back to his old school and attended classes.

Another glance out the window brought a happy surprise. Bill was getting out of a bright red Jeep along with Robert Ruskin. Janice experienced a momentary flashback. Had it only been last October when she stood on this very spot and watched Bill get out of a bright red sports car? That day fear and anger had gripped her at the appearance of her ex-husband after ten years of separation. Now she could hardly wait to get her arms around him.

"Bill! What a neat surprise! What brought you up here today? Is everything okay on the movie? Oh, your beard tickles!" Janice giggled, enjoying the warmth of Bill's embrace as she looked beyond him to include Ruskin in her greeting. "Hi, Rob."

"Hey, Janice. It's great to see you," the actor said. "Buck, this girl oughta be in movies."

"No way, Rob. I'm keeping her all to myself," Bill said. "Wow, sweetheart, I didn't realize how much I missed you." He lifted her off the floor and swung her around.

"Bill, I'm so glad you came," Janice said as soon as he put her down. "I'm worried about Billy . . . and Eric." She looked at Ruskin, then back at Bill. "They've been gone for hours on those stupid . . . those trail bikes."

The two men exchanged looks. Ruskin coughed and pursed his lips.

"Now, honey," Bill said, "boys will be boys. They're probably having the time of their lives and just didn't pay attention to the time."

"But you'd think they'd be hungry by now," she said.

"Believe me, Janice," Ruskin said, "when Eric gets hungry, he'll be back."

"Hey, you asked me why we're here," Bill said, wanting to divert the conversation away from her fears. "There was a problem on the set. One of the actors, you remember Milo Baker . . . he was . . . well, let's just say he had to drop out due to health concerns. We have to wait until the people who do the casting find someone who looks enough like him from a distance to fill the part."

"So," Janice said, delighted, "you came here to be with us." She gave Bill another hug, then pulled him over to a corner table. "You men sit down, and I'll get you something to eat. Do you want hamburgers, chili, steaks? What will it be . . . Oh, Bill!" She had stopped suddenly and was staring off at nothing in particular.

Bill and Robert Ruskin looked out the window to see if the boys had come back, but no one was there.

"Bill, I just had a wonderful idea. Rob, what would you think . . . I mean, would it be possible . . . Listen, I know an actor who's built just like Milo Baker. He's tall and rugged and can do an authentic western accent."

"Where did you meet an actor—at the grocery store?" Bill teased.

"No, silly. Right at our own building back home. It's Hal, the doorman." She frowned as the two men exchanged looks. "But listen, he's not just a doorman. He has studied acting and has done some movie and TV work. He'd really be good—I know he would. Oh, Rob, please give him a chance." She deliberately failed to mention that he'd only been an extra.

"Janice . . ." Bill began.

"No, Buck, that's okay. I'll call casting right now. It's the least I can do for Janice for helping me out with Eric. If this guy doesn't work out for wagonmaster, we can put him in the wagon train somewhere." Ruskin pulled a cellular phone from his pocket and dialed the long-distance number. "Hey, baby, this is Rob. Yeah, I'm cooling my heels. How's your search for my wagonmaster going? Okay. Well, listen, I have a lead for you. Try Hal . . . Hal . . . Janice, what's this guy's last name?"

Janice and Bill exchanged looks. "Oh dear, I don't know," she said, shrugging and shaking her head.

"You can call the condo office," Bill suggested. He pulled an address book from his pocket and gave the number to Ruskin, who repeated it to the casting agent on the phone.

"I hope it works out for your friend," Ruskin said to Janice after concluding his call. "Really. Hey, look who's here."

Two twelve-year-old boys barged in the front of the diner, their unbuttoned coats hanging half off their shoulders, their faces shining.

"What a trip!" Billy said.

"Yeah, it was something else!" Eric agreed. "Food! Give me food! Hey . . . Dad?"

"Hey, Buck!" Billy shouted. "Wow, we've been having a great time! Thanks for the trail bike. It's fantastic."

The boys and their fathers exchanged handshakes and shoulder slaps, then sat down at the table for lunch. A few customers entered the diner, but lunch business was much slower than breakfast and supper. Frankie served up some steaming chili for the group along with some of Mac's mile-high Mexican cornbread.

"Dad, can we go back down with you and take our bikes?" Eric asked. "We wouldn't get in the way, I promise."

"Yeah, can we, Buck?" Billy asked. "I'd like to try them out on some really rocky terrain."

Janice grimaced and opened her mouth to protest, but Ruskin spoke first.

"Well, we *are* planning to take you back with us. That's one reason we came today. But those bikes won't work down there. Actually, it's *up* there . . . southwest of here, but at a higher altitude. Snow still covers most of the area, and we get some new snow every few nights. That's why I chose that location."

Janice hoped she could thwart his plan. "Wouldn't they be in the way? Besides, tomorrow Scott and Kate will be coming over from Kansas, and they might take you boys back to their ranch for a visit. How would you like that?"

"Scott Lansing?" Eric almost shouted, "The Mavericks' MVP? Man, I don't want to miss seeing him."

"Me either," Billy added.

"I'd almost forgotten they were coming," Bill said. "I guess I've been concentrating so much on the film, it slipped my mind. Honey, how long did you say they're going to be here?"

"Just two days. I made arrangements for them to stay at the motel," Janice said.

"Sweetheart," Bill said, "how can you put someone like Scott Lansing in a dumpy motel like . . . ?" Her frown stopped him for a moment. "I'm sorry, but that's what it is."

"I've known the Willmans for over ten years, and they are very decent people. They've been repairing and repainting two adjoining rooms for the past three weeks just to get ready. You can't imagine what having a famous football player stay there means to them. Oh, Bill, you know Kate and Scott. They're the least pretentious people in the world. They won't mind a couple of nights in a little motel. Besides, it's all set." She lifted her chin slightly. She was getting tired of the way he looked down on her old neighborhood.

Bill sighed and shrugged. "I think I've lost control," he said to Ruskin, who was watching with a smile of amusement.

"Yeah, Buck, I think you have. Like I've told you, your story is going to be my next project. I can see the promo now. 'Big town Maverick lassoed and tamed by small-town filly.'"

Janice stood up abruptly and began clearing the table. "You'd better be joking," she said, tossing her hair over her shoulder and marching toward the kitchen with an armload of dishes.

Further problems on the set required Ruskin's immediate return, but Bill stayed with his family and waited for the Lansings' arrival. Bill and Janice used the time to solidify plans with the Devines for the expansion of their business.

"Instead of adding on, why not just build a new restaurant next to it?" Bill said. "Then you can move right in without interrupting service to your regular customers and tear down the old building afterwards."

"But this old building is practically a landmark," Gracie protested. "Folks expect to see it as they drive by."

"Maybe that's why they drive on by," Mac said. "I agree with Buck. Let's get a whole new look to this place."

Gracie scowled and opened her mouth to protest, then changed her mind and remained quiet.

Janice smiled. Usually Gracie would argue for the sake of arguing, but the Lord had already made a difference in the older woman's behavior.

"Well, I'll miss it, but you do what you think is best," Gracie said.

Mac stared at his wife, still not used to her new, softer responses. "On the other hand, maybe we ought to play up this landmark thing," he said.

Frankie sighed with exasperation. "Buck, you wouldn't believe it. My folks used to hardly ever agree on anything, but they always got things done. Now they're trying to outdo each other by giving in on everything, and *nothing* gets done."

Bill and Janice laughed.

"Then maybe you'd better make the decision," Bill said.

Frankie eyed his parents. They exchanged looks, then smiled and nodded to their son.

"Well, I go for the new look, Buck. And I can't hardly think of enough words to thank you."

"You're welcome," Bill said. "And that's enough of that. Let's get a contractor on this right away. We can open before Memorial Day if all goes well."

The Lansings arrived mid-morning and, true to Janice's prediction, were quite satisfied with the accommodations in the motel. After a hearty lunch in the diner, they joined the Masons in the large motor home Bill had rented for Janice and the boys to stay in while he was on location.

"Miss Janice," five-year-old Amy Lansing said as she nestled into Janice's arms, "I lost my front tooth." She opened her mouth wide to prove it.

"Miss Janice, I got my own pony," Amy's twin brother Sean said, determined not to be outdone by his sister.

"I got one, too, and besides, we're going to have a baby sister," Amy said.

"We are not. We're gonna have a baby brother," Sean said.

"Oh, Kate, how wonderful!" Janice said, "Bill, isn't that wonderful?"

Bill nodded pleasantly, but his expression told her he wasn't getting the same idea she was.

"Congratulations," he said to Scott. "You're going to have a whole bunkhouse full of little cowpokes, eh?"

Scott laughed. "Yep, and now I'll be home to raise 'em." He put his arm around Kate and pulled her closer to him on the couch. "Speaking of bunkhouses, we're building a half-dozen three-bedroom houses for the kids we're planning to bring out there. It took some time, but we finally decided what we want to do. Instead of giving just a few city kids a summer vacation, we've decided to give the most needy boys a permanent home. We'll have a married couple in every house to raise them like their own. It's worked for other ranches, and I think it will work for us."

"Most of all," Kate said, "it will finally give us a chance to minister like we've always wanted to. Teaching Sunday school, while it's a wonderful, much-needed ministry we'll keep on doing, never quite seemed enough. We've always hungered to do more. In a way, I was always scared that if I said yes to God, He'd send us to some remote corner of the world. But when I finally said, 'Not my will but Thine,' He plopped us right down on the very farm where I grew up. Sure goes to show you, He always does what's best. We just have to trust Him."

Scott poked his wife's side gently. "Sermon over?"

"That was not a sermon," Kate said. "That was a testimony."

"I'm proud of you, Scott, but I have to tell you, I'm going to hate not having you to receive for me. You make my worst passes look good," Bill said lightly. But inwardly his emotions churned as he tried to dodge the conviction Kate's words had created.

"Thanks, Buck," Scott said. "I can't say I won't miss football, but I will definitely not miss being pounded into the ground for a living. Hey, I almost forgot. Kate, you were supposed to remind me. Buck, here's a little present for you from Ryan Brooks and the Los Angeles Mavericks. They were real sorry you couldn't make it out for the ceremony last week when we all got ours." He reached in his coat pocket and pulled out a small velvet box.

Bill opened it as once again his emotions bordered on overload. It was his Super Bowl ring. He studied the giant ring, turning it around in his hands. Since the team colors were blue and silver, the men had chosen to have a large, perfectly symmetrical star sapphire set in gleaming platinum, with three diamonds on each side of the center stone.

He read the inscription, "Super Bowl Champions," and a hollow ache filled his heart. The day he had lived for since childhood had been so close to being his, but one moment of foolish pride, one moment of staying on the field when he didn't need to, giving Jared Hammer a chance to hit him one more, nearly fatal time, and his dream had been snatched from him, perhaps forever. The ring would now be a reminder of that mistake instead of the precious trophy it was meant to be.

As he turned the ring around again, his eyes caught something. At one point of the star, deep within the stone, was a minute black dot. For a moment he was angry that the jewelers had given him a less than perfect gem, but a second thought replaced that impulse. *How fitting*, he decided bitterly. The tiny black mark would forever be a symbol of his failure at the high point of his career. Not only that, but Ryan Brooks, who lived less than a two-hour drive from here, had sent the ring with Scott. Like a clever move in a chess game, Brooks's ploy of avoiding a private, personal encounter with Bill could only signify the Mavericks management's desire to keep next season's contract demands under their control.

Bill shoved the ring onto his middle finger next to his wedding band, then took it off and put it back in the black velvet box.

"I can't wear this thing while I'm making a movie. Janice, would you stick it in a drawer, please?"

The startled expressions on Scott's and Kate's faces made Bill regret his emphatic tone, and a new emotion added itself to the stew bubbling inside him: shame. How could he be concerned about football and contracts when these two wonderful people had just announced with all humility the full surrender of their lives into the hands of God? How could he fail to be grateful for all that God had done to bring Janice and Billy back into his life? How could he be so very bitter against God?

But he was.

Fourteen

JANICE PEERED OUT of the broad picture window of the motor home and smiled, happy for once to see Bill playing football. Billy and Eric had begged Scott and Bill for a game of tag football on the windswept field behind the diner, and the two men had gladly complied. While the twins and Junior Devine napped, Janice visited with Alice and Kate in the large, well-equipped vehicle that was her temporary home.

"Sure beats that old thing you used to live in," Alice said, looking around the room. "Oh, there I go again. I'm sorry, Jan. I guess I'm just a little bit jealous. Lord, forgive me."

"I'm the one who's jealous," Janice said. "You and Kate are so lucky to be expecting. I wish I could get the message across to Bill in some subtle way, but for an intelligent man, he sure seems dense on that subject."

Kate laughed. "Silly girl, just tell him you want a baby."

Janice cleared her throat. "Well, I would, but there are some things we just don't talk about." She saw the troubled looks on their faces. "Oh, don't worry, everything's okay. Really, it is. But we had some big arguments right after we got married . . ." She stopped. "You know, I've never talked to anyone like this. I shouldn't have said that."

"Oh, Janice, honey," Kate said, "all couples argue. It just takes time and patience to learn how to work out your differences without quarreling, at least in a hurtful way. Scott and I still bicker, but we have ground rules that keep it from damaging our relationship."

Alice nodded. "Me and Frankie, too. But I wonder if there's not something else eating at you."

"Alice is right." Kate said. "Something is going on here, and we need to talk about it."

Janice looked at her doubtfully. It seemed disloyal to talk about Bill behind his back, but how else could she get the answers to the questions that troubled her?

"Let me make it easy for you," Kate said. "For the short time I've known you and the long time I've known Buck, I think I can see what's going on. He's mad at God about the Super Bowl, so he hasn't been reading his Bible or praying, right?"

Janice nodded, and her eyes began to sting as tears formed. After a guilty glance out the window, she said, "He's really wonderful. I love him so much, I can hardly believe it sometimes. And I know he loves me. I overheard him telling Robert Ruskin he couldn't be in the movie if Angela Bains was in it. I guess he realized I was a little jealous that he used to date her, so he was willing to give the movie up to prove he loves me. That really meant a lot to me. But still, he's different from . . . from before his injury. When he first showed up here last fall, I hated to hear him talk about God, but once I became a Christian, I couldn't get enough. Remember, Alice?"

Her friend nodded. "We had some great talks then too."

"Bill would call me long-distance every few days and answer any question I had about the Bible. Lately when I've asked him something, he either pretends not to hear me or says he'll look it up later. But he never does, so I've stopped asking." Janice pulled a tissue from her pocket and wiped away the tears rolling down her cheeks.

Kate put her arm around Janice's shoulders, and Alice patted her hand.

"Do you think he doesn't want to be a Christian anymore?" Janice asked, looking from one friend to the other.

Kate glanced at Alice, then gave Janice another hug. "Honey, he doesn't have any say-so about that. The Bible says that once you become a child of God, no one, not even you yourself, can snatch you out of God's hand. I know for sure Buck is a Christian. He's just acting like a spoiled child . . . not that I have any room to talk—it takes one to know one . . . but he's still *God's* child."

"That's right," Alice said. "And don't you worry, Jan, he's gonna come around one of these days. We've already been praying about it, me and Frankie."

"Just look at him out there," Kate said. "That big old woolly black beard sure makes him look like a pioneer preacher, doesn't it? Maybe the Lord will use this movie part to turn him around."

"That would be the easy way, wouldn't it?" Janice said.

Alice grinned. "Can I ask a question and you won't think I'm rude?"

"Go ahead," Janice said.

"Does it tickle when he kisses you?"

Janice and Kate laughed at the way Alice wrinkled her nose as she asked the question, welcoming a humorous thought to lighten their serious discussion.

"Sort of," Janice said. "It scratched like crazy until he got about two weeks' growth. Now it's really kind of a soft tickle." She felt like a schoolgirl telling secrets, but the warmth of these new friendships quickly soothed away any guilty thoughts.

As Bill, Scott, and the boys returned to the motor home and the smaller children woke up from their naps, the three women began preparing snacks in the small but deluxe kitchen area.

"Don't you worry, Jan," Alice said, "you can count on me and Frankie to keep on praying for you and Buck. It's gonna turn out okay."

"Scott and I will be praying too," Kate said. "In fact, I can't see Scott letting this go on for too much longer. He's about to lose patience with his old buddy. I'll bet you a dime to a jelly bean he sits Buck down for a big brother talk one day soon."

As the men opened the door, and a fresh breeze blew into the room, Janice heaved an involuntary sigh of relief. What a comfort it was to have friends who cared enough to listen, pray, and help! This was living proof of the love and acceptance Dr. Miller, her mother, Kate, and even the Christian woman in the secondhand store had talked about. By experiencing it, she was finally beginning to understand.

That afternoon Scott invited Bill to ride along as he drove the twenty miles into Pueblo to look for some farm equipment. Billy and Eric were eager to ride their trail bikes again and didn't ask to go along, but the twins begged to accompany their father and were appeased only with promises of a visit to the movie set the next day.

"This has been a rough few months for you, hasn't it, Buck?" Scott said as he drove his shiny new oversized pickup away from the diner.

Bill glanced at his friend, then back out the window at the barren, windswept plain. He should have known better than to get alone with Scott. Now he was sure to hear some preaching.

"Come on, Buck, this is your old pal Scott. Let's talk. What's going on?"

An old familiar warmth sprang unbidden in Bill's chest. What was the matter with him? Scott was the best friend he'd ever had. He'd understand more than anybody about the awful confusion and pain Bill felt.

"I'm not sure what next season holds for me. It's not just the usual contract hassles. There's something missing—the power, the strength, that deep-down feeling that I can do anything. I'm not sure I'm going to make it back next season."

Scott shot him a glance. "Would it make that much difference?"

"Football is my life, Scott. I love the game. I've lived for it since I was old enough to play peewee games as a kid. What else would I ever want to do?"

"I'd say farming and ranching, like me, but that's not your style. But it seems to me you have a big-time movie career coming along right now."

Bill shrugged. "It's pretty decent, but I haven't really gotten on my feet in it yet. Besides, I wanted to move into it slowly so it would be there when my football days were over. I never thought it would happen this soon."

"That happens to everybody, me included. I know what you mean about not feeling the strength. There was one time last season when I got hit real bad . . ."

"The Raiders game?"

"Yeah." Scott laughed. "Man, I thought I'd die right there. I can remember thinking, 'Lord, take me now, I can't stand the pain.' Somehow I knew right then that it was stupid to go on playing football when I had a family to raise. What's so macho about getting beat up like that when there's real honest work that can change people's lives?"

"Some people would say you lost your nerve."

"And some people would say when you reach the top, move over and let someone else play the game."

Bill gave a bitter snort, and Scott immediately regretted his words.

"Yeah," Bill said. "Well, I haven't reached the top, not yet. And I may never get another chance. Look, I know how stupid I was to not listen to you in that game with the Aces. We were beating them into the ground, and you told me to let Joey finish the game. But I wouldn't listen. I had to prove something. If I'd just listened, Hammer never would have hit me that last time, I'd still be playing, and . . ."

"And it would have been your Super Bowl instead of Joey's?"

"Unh!!" An angry grunt exploded from Bill, and he slapped the padded dashboard of the pickup with his fist, venting at last all the feelings he'd been trying to bury for months. "How could I have been so stupid?" he shouted.

To his amazement, in the silence that followed his outburst he felt a strange sense of relief, followed by mild annoyance. On the one hand, it felt good to talk to the one friend who truly understood him. On the other hand, he knew Scott was over there behind the wheel driving up the road just praying like crazy that his old buddy Buck would get straightened out with the Lord. After staring out the window for several minutes, he looked at Scott and saw his neutral expression. Maybe he wouldn't preach at him after all.

Scott glanced in his direction. "Since I'm driving, I know you won't throw me out of the truck when I remind you that way back last fall you said that you'd give up football if you could have your wife and son back."

Bill frowned. Had he really said that? He had more than said it—he had prayed it. He had offered to God the *career* he loved so he could have the two *people* he loved more than anything in the world. But why did it have to be a choice?

"Of course, I don't believe for a minute that God makes us choose things that way," Scott said, as if he'd read Bill's mind. "I just thought I'd remind you. Hey, here we are."

He drove the pickup into the parking lot of a giant tractor warehouse store.

Bill tagged along as Scott made a pretense of shopping for farm equipment. It was clear this short trip into Pueblo had been arranged so they could talk, and Bill had to admit to himself that he did feel a little better.

The double-seated crew cab of the pickup was filled to capacity as it sped down the highway toward the Rancho

Grande de Montoya. Scott and Kate were fulfilling their promise to take the twins to the movie location and also returning Bill to work. Billy and Eric had opted to spend a few days on the set rather than go to Kansas. And Janice was looking forward to seeing her old friend Hal who would hopefully be in the movie because of her recommendation.

"I sure hope it works out for him," she told Bill.

"Yeah, me, too," he said. "It'll be pretty embarrassing if he's a dud."

"Bill, that's mean!" Janice lifted his arm from around her shoulders and gave him a little shove. "The poor man has been trying to get into movies for years. I just want him to have a chance to succeed."

"Hmmm," Bill said, putting his arm back around her and giving her a squeeze. "Do I have cause for a little jealousy here?"

She gave him a saucy grin. "Bill, don't be silly. He's old enough to be my father. I just like him, that's all. He's a really nice, lonely old man who gave up everything for his career, including his family, but sadly, nothing ever came of it."

Bill shifted uncomfortably in his seat, annoyed by this parallel between his life and the would-be-actor doorman. Years ago he too had forgotten his family just so he could build his career. Now God had given him back his family. He knew he should be grateful for that—and far more charitable toward Hal.

"If it means that much to you, I hope he succeeds too." He pulled her close again and kissed the top of her head. As always, the sweet fragrance of her hair and the warmth of her slender body soothed his troubled spirit.

The set was alive with activity, and the arrival of Bill's group caused even more. Many of the film crew were Mavericks fans and were eager to welcome Bill back and to meet Scott. Billy and Eric raced to check out the stunt being prepared on a nearby hillside. Kate kept a tight rein on her active twins to keep them from getting into trouble.

"Mrs. Mason! Mrs. Mason!" Hal hurried over to the pickup

as its passengers went their different ways. His three-day growth of beard had been enhanced by a makeup artist, and his scruffy costume gave him the look of a rough-and-ready wagon train leader. His glasses had been replaced with contact lenses, and despite the gray streaks in his shaggy wig, he looked years younger than he had only a few weeks ago.

Janice reached out her hand to shake his. "Hal, I'm so happy to see . . ." She paused for a moment. Why did he suddenly remind her of someone else—and who? His eyes and brow line, now that his glasses were gone—the slope of his shoulders—the boyish turn of his head as he grinned in open appreciation.

She suddenly saw in her mind her poor, long-dead brother Peter. *Thanks for sewing my button on, Sis. Mom was, well, you know, she wasn't feeling too good.* Why should she think now about Peter and the simple favor she'd done for him so long ago?

"I can never thank you enough for getting me this job, ma'am," he said. "I've already had my screen test, and Ruskin thinks I'm right for the part. I owe it all to you."

"Hey, big Hal," Bill greeted, taking his turn to shake the man's hand. "Welcome to the cast."

"Thanks, Mr. Mason," Hal responded.

"That's Buck to you," Bill said. "No formalities here. Scott, let me introduce you to our friend Hal . . . Hal . . . What's your last name? I don't recall ever hearing it."

"It's Griffin, Buck—Albert Griffin. Pleased to meet you, Mr. Lansing," he said, shaking hands with Scott.

"First names, Hal," Scott replied. "Remember?"

"Thank you, sir," Hal said, unable to easily put aside his doorman status. "Mrs. Mason, I mean, Janice . . . Excuse me, ma'am, are you all right? You're as white as a ghost."

Janice leaned against Bill, her head light and her legs threatening to buckle.

"Who are you?" she whispered. "Are you . . . ?"

"Why, ma'am, I'm Hal Grif . . ."

"Albert Griffin . . . from Theodore, Alabama."

"Why, yes, ma'am. I did live in Theodore for a few years. But that was nearly twenty-nine, thirty years ago. How did you know?"

"Bill, get me out of here," Janice whispered, burying her face in his chest and bursting into tears.

"Man, this is really weird," Bill said, suddenly understanding. "Hal, we grew up in Theodore. Janice never knew her father, but his name was . . . Albert Griffin. That has to be you. You were married to Margaret Griffin, right?"

Hal nodded wordlessly.

"Then you're Janice's father."

"What?" Hal said. "Man, I don't . . ."

"Bill, get me away from him." Janice grasped the front of Bill's coat and looked at him with pleading eyes.

"But, sweetheart," Bill said softly, "this is your father. Isn't it incredible that the very man you wanted to help turns out to be your own father?"

"Don't you understand?" she whispered through clenched teeth. "He deserted us. He left and never said a word. My mother nearly died from alcoholism, and my brother Peter *did* die. And he never knew, he never cared, he forgot us as if we'd never existed."

She tried to bury her tear-streaked face in his chest again, but he gently grasped her chin and stared into her eyes. The agony in his face revealed much more than empathy.

"Just like me," he whispered.

Janice gasped. "No, not like you. Like . . ."

"You only say that because you've forgiven me," he said.

Understanding flickered in her eyes, but she shook her head to quench it. "He left us . . ."

"Like you left your mother," Bill said.

She winced, then glanced at the older man. His dumbfounded, fear-filled expression sent a flash of rage through her. Apparently this turn of events had merely frightened him, as though he were afraid of losing his part in the movie and that was it. Janice looked back at Bill. "I can't . . ."

"Sweetheart, I won't pretend to understand everything that's going on here. All I can say is that somehow God has brought your father back into your life . . ." Bill stopped, surprised at his own words.

Janice was equally surprised. She stared into his face with a sudden, quivering smile. If that man's reentry into her life caused Bill to talk about God again, she would not do anything to discourage it. She turned slowly toward Albert Griffin, uncertain what she would or could say.

"Well, I suppose we have a lot to catch up on, Hal. About twenty-nine years' worth." Janice took a deep breath to control her churning emotions. When Hal's face relaxed and he gave a nervous laugh, her anger mixed with disgust. How else would she expect this pathetic, desperate old man to react? She remembered the time when she'd recently tried to talk to him about the Lord and how quickly he'd changed the subject. As confused as she'd been about that encounter, she was certain God had told her to talk to Hal. Now she understood why. This wayward sinner, her delinquent father, was about to get saved. But somehow that didn't seem as important to her as his getting what he deserved. He had no idea of the regret and remorse, especially about her brother's death, she was about to unload on him. How odd that she felt a sense of vengeance toward him rather than pity. How strange that she would just as soon see him stay unsaved!

Fifteen

BILL PACED HIS TRAILER, going over his lines again and again. It had been difficult to shut out the drama going on in Janice's life and concentrate on his acting, but things had finally settled down. As planned, Billy and Eric had stayed with their fathers. Disappointed with their choice, Janice had ridden back to the diner with the Lansings, who needed to return to their ranch. Bill wanted her to stay with him but knew she found it difficult to be near Hal, especially after Billy had so readily accepted his grandfather.

So far Bill's scenes had gone well. Although Ruskin was the star as well as the director of the film, Bill had an important secondary role. His character was a pivotal influence in the life of the main character, John Martin. And just yesterday he, Buck Mason, pro football player, star quarterback, had discovered that he could really act. This newfound awareness had both invigorated and empowered him as he portrayed his character.

The obscure missionary pioneer Angus MacGuinness had brought his wife, Clare, to Colorado in the years following the Civil War. Along the way, they discovered she was expecting their first child, but it was too late to turn back. In addition to the hardships endured by all settlers of the West, the wagon train in which they traveled was struck with smallpox just as they reached the town of Placer, later called Russell. Immune to the disease because of earlier exposure, Angus and Clare selflessly nursed John Martin and others back to health but buried many others. But then Clare became ill with pneumonia.

Bill was deeply touched by the story. He and Angie Paine, the actress who was playing his wife, had an amiable relationship, and she was able to help him avoid overdramatizing his character. Just the day before, she'd pulled a practical joke on him after a tense scene, and he had welcomed the comic relief. But today he would be playing his most dramatic scene, and despite his growing confidence in his acting ability, he wondered if he could pull it off.

"Hey, Buck," Billy called as he and Eric burst through the trailer door just ahead of Bill's assistant. "Ready on the set!"

The two boys plopped on the couch, laughing at the assistant, who was shaking his head in mock annoyance.

"Five minutes, Buck," Jason said. "By the way, there's a wind coming up, so you'd better wear your coat to the set."

"Can we watch the scene?" Billy asked.

"Naw, that's boring," Eric said. "I have something else planned."

"You two stay out of trouble," Bill said. "Billy, I promised your mother . . ."

"Aw, Buck, she wouldn't let me walk across the street if she had her way." Billy grinned at his father, then shot a mischievous look at Eric.

Bill pointed his finger at his son. "You stay out of trouble." Then he chuckled. Billy was the last kid in the world who needed to be told that. "I'll tell you what—as soon as we finish this next scene, the three of us will take off and find some action."

"Cool!" said Billy.

"You got it!" said Eric.

As soon as Bill stepped out of the trailer, Eric walked to the door to be sure they were alone. Only then did he pull a bundle out of his coat pocket.

"Look at what I have."

Curious about his pal's treasure, Billy jumped up from the couch. "What is it? Aw, come on, Eric. Not cigarettes. That's too dumb, even for you." Billy hoped his mild teasing would help him avoid a confrontation with his friend.

"These aren't just any cigarettes. They have a special kick, if you know what I mean." Eric cocked his head and gave Billy a knowing look.

Billy cleared his throat and looked down at his feet. "Where'd you get them?"

"From one of the . . . Never mind where. Come on, little Buck." Eric jerked his head toward the door. "Let's find our own action." He nervously glanced out the window before opening the door. "You coming?"

Billy's heart was in his throat. "No," he said softly.

Eric glared at him. "Sissy."

"No," Billy said more firmly, lifting his chin and glaring back.

Eric dropped his angry stare first. Then he sighed, almost with relief, and shook his head. "I just wanted to try them. I've never really done drugs. Honest."

Billy sighed with relief too. "Me neither. I have an idea. Let's make a pact, okay? We won't ever start. And if one of us even thinks about it, we'll call the other one so he can talk us out of it. Okay?"

Eric considered the proposal for only a moment. "You got it."

The two boys shook hands and slapped each other's shoulder.

"I do have another idea," Eric said. "And this one is okay. Remember the snowmobiles they're using to get to some of the remote areas for stunts and stuff?"

"Yeah, what about them?"

"They're a lot like our trail bikes. I've ridden them bunches of times. Let's go take a ride—just a short one around the hills. It's okay. Really it is. My dad owns this movie and everything to do with it, remember?"

Billy frowned. At the risk of Eric's friendship, he'd stood up to him about the drugged cigarettes. It couldn't hurt to take a snowmobile ride.

"Get rid of the cigarettes," he said.

Eric pulled them from his pocket once more and started to drop them in the trash can.

"Not here, stupid," Billy said. "You want to get my dad in trouble? Dump them outside someplace. Wait a minute while I grab a couple of snack bars from my dad's stash."

Typical for late-April weather in the mountains of Colorado, the cold spring wind sent icy gusts through the wagon train in the shadowed valley. Clouds had been gathering all day, and a hint of moisture in the usually dry air suggested that it might snow again by nightfall.

Bill shivered despite his coat, trying to get warm after his last, unsuccessful take. Annoyed with himself that he couldn't get it right so they could wrap up the day's shoot, he eyed Robert Ruskin, who was giving instructions to the camera crew. Bill knew the director was repeating himself to the experienced cameramen, taking out on them his frustration with Bill. Ruskin always tried to avoid upsetting his actors. However, with the weather cold enough to cause an actor to shiver realistically for this important scene, he wanted it in the can *today*.

For Bill, this scene was different from the rest. It was one thing to act or react in dialogue with other actors, playing off their lines and movements. It was another thing to recite a monologue, and worse still, a *prayer*, taken from the diary of a long-dead missionary. It had been so long since Bill had prayed, he couldn't even find any inner resources to tap into.

Ruskin sauntered toward him, looking up at the cloudy sky and scratching his beard. "I don't know about you, Buck, but I can't wait to get rid of this thing."

Bill grunted his agreement. He knew this was only a disjointed preamble.

Ruskin cleared his throat. "I'm not sure how to say this, Buck, but . . . First of all, we both know the scene's not working. Just yesterday you had it in the bag. What's the matter . . . No, I want to tell you something else first. I just want you to know how much I appreciate your not cramming your religion down my throat. I didn't grow up religious, and I'm not sure I see any value in it. But I do admire the people we're portraying here, and I admire you. You're a real and sincere person. Now listen to me . . . This is the only way I can tell you what I want you to do. Play it like you're talking to God . . . like He's an actual person and a close friend, someone you really know. My second wife used to do that, and it drove me crazy. But that's what I want you to do."

The director finished in a rush, as though his words were tripping over themselves. Having finished, he nodded his head curtly to Bill and turned around.

"Places, everybody. Let's get it right this time."

Bill swallowed hard as Ruskin's words burned into his soul. The man had spoken eternal truth and didn't even realize it. God *was* a real Person and a close friend. How could Bill have ever forgotten that? And how had Ruskin managed to see something of Bill's "religion" when Bill had virtually shut down that part of his life? No wonder he'd only been able to say these lines like a memorized speech.

His heart in his throat, he handed his coat to his assistant and moved into position, kneeling beside a broken wagon wheel. The makeup man stepped close to drop artificial tears in his eyes, but Bill shook his head.

"Quiet on the set. Action!"

Bill blinked his eyes, and tears splashed down his cheeks—real, warm tears that turned icy in the wind before they reached his beard.

"Oh, God, loving Father, forgive me. Forgive my willfulness

in insisting that Clare come with me to establish this mission instead of my taking her back to Westport until the baby came. Don't take her away from me, please, God. I need her more than I need life itself. I won't demand anything from her again, or from You, if You'll just let her . . . and our precious son . . . live."

Bill paused, looked down, shuddered, then raised his eyes again. "Oh, God, my self-centeredness is revealed even in that prayer. So many have died for the sake of Your Gospel. How can I bargain with You who gave Your only Son for me? Help me let go. Help me surrender my will to You. Oh, Lord, no prayer will ever be harder for me, but I mean it with all my heart." After another pause, he whispered, "Not my will, but Thine be done."

As the camera moved back, Ruskin limped slowly toward Bill and laid a hand on his shoulder. "She's asking for you, Preacher."

Bill looked up, then stood, and the two men walked through the snow toward another wagon.

"Cut!" Ruskin shouted. "Buck, that was it! That was perfect. Have you got it, Hank?"

"Got it," the cameraman answered.

Barely aware of his surroundings, Bill walked through the maze of cameras, equipment, and people, returned to the privacy of his trailer, and sat with his head in his hands.

"Lord, I'm such a hypocrite," he prayed, *really* prayed, for the first time in months. "No wonder I had so much trouble with those lines. At least when Angus MacGuinness tried to bargain with You, it was for his mission, for people's *souls*, not for a self-gratifying career like football. He buried his wife and son and died when he was younger than I am now. But You've given me back my wife and son—and my own life."

Bill looked up, not seeing the textured ceiling of his trailer. "Lord, my whole life has always been about me and what I want. But now I understand what You've been trying to tell me. Lord, You can have the Super Bowl, and You can have football. Like

Angus, like Kate Lansing, and like my Lord Jesus Christ prayed, 'Not my will, but Thine be done.'"

A flash of sunshine broke through the late-afternoon clouds and shone through the window of the trailer, bringing warmth and peace to Bill's heart. He had a sudden urge to phone Janice and tell her all about the scene that had moved him so deeply. Dear, sweet Janice, waiting patiently for him to get his spiritual life straightened out. He'd put her through a lot these past four months. He would promise her that they didn't have to live in California if she didn't want to. And he would stop pretending not to hear her hints about wanting another baby. Another baby would be great! And then there was Billy, who wasn't even saved. Bill regretted all the time he'd wasted!

Bill grabbed the phone and began punching numbers, but a knock on the door interrupted him.

"Buck, have you seen the boys?" Ruskin stuck his head into the trailer. "I can't find Eric anyplace."

"No," Bill said. "Have you checked with Hal Griffin? Billy's been hanging around him for the past few days."

"They're not with me," Hal said from behind Ruskin.

"What I'm saying is, I can't find either of the boys," Ruskin said. "They aren't anywhere on the movie set."

Figuring they'd probably just wandered off somewhere but somehow knowing something worse had occurred, Bill grabbed his coat and flung it on as he jumped down the two steps of the trailer, slamming the door behind him. Was this what surrender to God brought, losing his son again?

"No!" he said beneath his breath. "I won't think that way. God, help us find the boys. No promises. No bargains. Just please help us find them, Lord. Please!"

Sixteen

BUT, MOTHER, HE DIDN'T even ask about you . . . or Peter." Janice paced the length of her motor home as she talked on a cordless phone. "I can understand his shock over finding out I'm his daughter since he didn't even know you were pregnant with me when he left. But *Peter* . . . his son!"

When Margaret Griffin didn't respond, Janice knew the mention of Peter, even eleven years after his death, was renewing her mother's heartache. Her mother was undoubtedly in shock over the discovery of her ex-husband. But after a moment Margaret merely sighed.

"It does seem strange, doesn't it, dear," she said. "But twenty-nine years is a long time. I'm sure a lot of things have happened in his life. He may even have had another family."

"No, he didn't. I asked him. I guess I wasn't very nice about it, but I told him he should see what a beautiful woman you are, what he missed out on by leaving you."

Margaret laughed. "Thank you, my dear. But you have to remember, I wasn't so lovely in my drinking days. And you do remember, don't you, Janice?"

It was Janice's turn to be quiet for a moment. "I have to admit, when I told him about Peter dying in that army training mission, he got choked up. Maybe that's why he's latched on to Billy."

"That poor child!" Margaret said. "He keeps having relatives pop out of the woodwork!"

Janice laughed. "I never even thought of that."

"Oh, honey, I know God is bringing us back together for some wonderful reason. Can't you see what an amazing miracle it is that your very own father was the doorman at your condominium, that in spite of how shy you can be sometimes, you struck up a friendship with him, and that you got him that part in the movie? Isn't that simply amazing?"

Janice marveled at her mother's loving acceptance of the situation. "I suppose so. And I guess that means I'd better try to like him. But I don't think I can call him Dad. It's funny, Mother, I felt so sorry for him back home in L.A. . . ." Janice paused. She hadn't thought of the condominium as home before. The word just popped out of her mouth, and somehow it seemed appropriate. Another thought struck her. "Mother, here I am so concerned about my feelings. How do *you* feel about all this? Please tell me you don't want to see him."

"Now, Janice . . ." Margaret said. "Besides, you did tell me he said he regretted giving up his family. That's a step in the right direction. And if he wants to see me, well, I've always been right here where he left me."

"Mother, you're too good," Janice said. "Oh, dear, I just looked at the clock . . . I hate to cut this short, but I promised Mac I'd come over and help tonight. Business is really booming. We'll talk more tomorrow, okay?"

"I'll look forward to it," Margaret said.

Janice grabbed a light jacket, then traded it for a warmer one before heading toward the diner. The cold spring wind cut through her jeans, reminding her that just four months of mild California weather had nearly spoiled her for Colorado. She hoped Bill was making their son wear his down-filled coat and heavy gloves.

The diner was filled with hungry truck drivers and tourists.

It took Janice and two other waitresses, plus both Frankie and Mac in the kitchen, to keep things running smoothly.

Janice tried to avoid the back corner table, but it was no use. Terrell Martin was there with several other drivers, and she dreaded seeing him again. But to her surprise, he smiled warmly when she approached to take their orders.

"Janice, it's good to see you. I want to introduce you to somebody. This here is Stacey Webb. She's gonna be driving the other truck for my new company, so I'm teaching her the route. We're hauling a load to Alamosa tonight." Terrell grinned, and his eyes seemed to sparkle as he looked at the young brunette beside him.

Janice tried not to smile too broadly as she shook hands with the newcomer. Though Stacey was seated, Janice could see she was tall and, being well-tanned and a little stocky, quite different from her.

"It's nice to meet you," Janice said.

"Me too," the woman said. "I've heard a lot about you."

Janice glanced at Terrell, who gave her a sheepish look and a wink. She shook her head and rolled her eyes. "What can I get for you all?"

"Janice," Frankie called across the busy room, "phone call. It's Buck."

"Excuse me," Janice said. "I'll only be a minute." She glanced again at Terrell and was pleased to see him nodding with assent at this unexpected interruption from Bill.

"Janice, I have some bad news," Bill said over the phone. "Billy and Eric have wandered off. They took one of the snowmobiles, so we don't know how far they went. There's new snow all over the place, so they're hard to track, even with the search team from the sheriff's department."

Janice leaned against the counter to keep from falling. She had trusted Bill with their son, and now he had lost him, just like he had last fall. But that had been in Denver, a city where Billy could find shelter, not on a snow-covered mountain with below-zero weather.

"Janice," Bill said frantically, "are you there?"

"Yes, I'm here."

"Honey, I need you. Please get Frankie to bring you down here right away."

"He can't," Janice whispered, trying to swallow the dreadful fear that was choking her.

"Janice, honey, what's wrong?" Frankie was suddenly there, his arm around her. "You're as white as death." He took the phone from her.

"Buck, what's going on?"

Bill repeated the story to Frankie. "Is there any way you can get her down here?"

Frankie studied Janice's face. "Does she really need to come, Buck? We can pray right here and take care of her . . . Uh, I mean . . ."

"I need to talk to her face to face, Frankie. I'm really scared, and I don't know how this is going to work out. But I know that if it's bad, we need to be together."

"We'll get her there. Somebody will," Frankie said. "It'll be less than two hours."

He hung up the phone, then hugged Janice and closed his eyes. "Lord, we've called on You to bring this family together, and that's what You've done. Now please bring Billy and his friend safely through this."

"What's going on?" Terrell Martin stood beside them, flanked by his friend Stacey.

Frankie told the story to Terrell and everyone else in the diner. "So if you're praying folks, we'd be much obliged if you'd pray for the boys."

"I'll do more than that," Terrell said. "I'm going down there to look for them. Anybody else?"

A dozen volunteers grabbed a last bite of food and their

coats and headed out the door. "Dinner's on the house," Mac said to those who tried to pay him.

"Come on, Janice. You can ride with us," Stacey said.

Inside the cab of the eighteen-wheeler, Janice shivered despite the warmth. Where was Billy? Did he have his coat on? What had possessed him to go off like that? Why hadn't Bill been watching him? Why hadn't Hal watched him? Why hadn't that Robert Ruskin watched his own son? It was probably Eric's fault. Billy knew better than to wander off in the mountains.

"Janice, it's going to be okay," Terrell said. "I bet they'll be there waiting for you when we get there."

"It's going to work out." Stacey put her arms around Janice.

They drove through the small town of Walsenburg and headed up the mountain toward La Veta Pass. Sparkling in the headlights, giant snowflakes fell lazily toward the wet highway until they were spun into a flurry by the passing vehicle. Janice stared into the darkness, trying to pray. Where was the peace that always came when she asked God for something? Was this cold, empty feeling a frightful sign that God wouldn't answer her prayer for her son's safety?

Bill stared at the distant searchlights as they danced a ghostly jig high up in the hills amid the lightly falling snow. As much as he longed to be up there with them, he had yielded to the sheriff's orders. Playing football, he had learned that every man has his job. The quarterback doesn't play defensive tackle. So when the Costilla County Sheriff's Department had called in experienced volunteers from the area, he reluctantly returned to wait near his trailer for Janice.

He approved of the sheriff's method of setting up a grid-like pattern to keep track of the experienced searchers as they lumbered across the mountain on snowshoes. It would be difficult to miss the boys with such a thorough system. But unfortunately, their only leads, the numerous crisscrossed snowmobile tracks, disappeared as the snow deepened. They couldn't be sure the boys had gone north from the movie location. And with the wind increasing and the temperature gradually dropping, how long could the searchers continue their quest?

Chilled to the bone, Bill sought refuge in his trailer where the location caterers had left a thermos of hot chocolate. As the hot liquid slid down his throat and warmed his whole body, he shuddered with pangs of guilt. How could he seek warmth for himself when his son might be freezing to death?

Death? Bill shuddered again.

"Oh, God, please give me another chance to witness to Billy. I've wallowed in self-pity and wasted all this time when I should have been telling him about You. And poor Eric, too, Lord. There are two boys out there who need You. Please save them."

Robert Ruskin knocked on the door and entered the trailer without waiting for a response. He was dripping with a mixture of wet snow and sweat.

"You're gonna get pneumonia that way, Rob," Bill said. "I'll page Jason and have him bring you a change of clothes."

"My assistant is bringing me a change," Ruskin said gruffly. He tossed off his coat and eased himself into a chair. "Look, I came to tell you that I'm . . . I'm ready to . . ." The word was difficult for him to say. ". . . to pray. Now don't get any ideas. I just figure it couldn't hurt. And none of this 'not my will, but Thine' stuff. I just want my boy back, and I want him back *now*."

Bill gave him a doubtful look. "Okay . . ." He stared at the floor, uncertain of what to say. Here they were, two men who'd always been in charge of their own lives as well as ordering others around in one way or another in their respective jobs. They were successful. They were rich. They were famous. And now they were completely powerless about what meant the most to them in the world—their sons.

"I'm being punished, you know," Ruskin said. "My second wife always said God was going to get me."

Bill gave a short cough. "I don't think she meant it that way, Rob. I think she meant . . ."

"Yeah, yeah. Whatever." Ruskin exploded with a heavy sigh, then sat back and ran his hand through his shaggy hair. He sat up again. "So how do we do this? Do we promise . . ." He cleared his throat. ". . . do we promise God that we'll give money to charity or stop smoking or . . ." He laughed bitterly. "Or give my ex-wives more alimony? Heaven knows I give them enough. Sorry. I didn't mean any disrespect." He slumped in his chair. "Just tell me what to do, Buck," he whispered.

Bill shook his head ruefully. "Rob, don't try to bargain with God. Just ask for His mercy, that's all. That's what I'm doing."

Billy rolled over in the snow and grabbed his leg, willing it not to hurt. Why did it have to be his left one that twisted as they crashed? He took a deep breath and forced out a laugh.

"Cool wipeout, eh, Eric?" he shouted over the whirring of the snowmobile motor.

The machine sputtered into a stall and then was silent.

"Eric?" Billy repeated. He grabbed a nearby boulder and pulled himself up, testing his leg. It hurt like crazy, but it wasn't broken again. He limped around the snowmobile, lying on its side, and found Eric facedown in the snow.

"Eric!" he shouted, pulling his friend over and cradling his head in his lap.

Blood oozed from a two-inch gash on Eric's forehead near the right temple, and a large bump was forming beneath it.

"Oooommmm," Eric moaned. "Ooowww!"

"It's okay," Billy said. "You're gonna be okay, Eric." Billy looked around frantically, trying to figure out what to do. The snow was beginning to come down faster now, and the temperature was dropping noticeably.

The boys had been on their way back to the movie set when they spied what looked like an old mine.

"It'll just take a minute to check it out," Eric had insisted. "We can come back tomorrow with flashlights for some serious exploring."

"Sure," Billy agreed, knowing full well the dangers of exploring mines. He hoped Buck would tell him he couldn't go. Otherwise, Eric would call him a sissy again.

Eric directed the snowmobile up a steep incline. But when he poured on the power, he misjudged a deep drift, and they crashed.

"My head hurts," Eric said now as he tried to sit up.

Billy lifted him to a sitting position. "You have a neat goose egg there," he said lightly. "And a little cut too. I have a handkerchief..."

Eric suddenly lurched to the side and vomited. Billy nearly followed suit.

"Gross! Come on, Eric, don't get disgusting on me," he said.

Eric rolled back against his friend. "I don't feel so good."

Billy wiped the blood away from Eric's face with his handkerchief. "Can you walk, Eric?" he said.

"I don't know."

"Just try." Billy helped Eric to stand, once again willing himself to ignore the pain in his left leg. It had hurt much worse when it was broken, and many times worse when he'd had surgery last fall. "This hill is pretty steep, Eric. If we kind of lie back and slide on the snow, we might be able to get down."

"Whatever you say." Eric gave Billy a dazed grin, then shook his head a little, trying to focus his eyes. "Ooowww!"

"Just take it easy," Billy said. Holding Eric up, he looked around for the best way down the hill. Snow covered all but a few boulders. He realized his plan just wouldn't work.

"Please, God," Billy said. "Please, God, please, God." He looked uphill. "I have a better idea, Eric! We'll take shelter in the mine. Then we can walk out in the morning when you feel better. I still have those candy bars . . ."

He half pushed, half dragged Eric through twenty yards of deep snow to the mine. Dirt, rocks, and broken beams partially covered the timber-braced opening, but they were able to crawl over them into the small cave-like space between the entrance and an inner solid barricade nearby. Although the outer opening had been broken down by would-be explorers, the inner barricade stood fast. Obviously, the owners didn't want this place explored.

They rested for a few moments before trying to talk. Billy watched Eric with fear and concern.

"Don't throw up again, okay?" he said. "I don't want you to stink things up."

Eric grinned. "I won't. I feel better now." He glanced around, his head wobbling. "Got any ideas about how we're gonna keep from freezing to death?"

Billy swallowed hard. In spite of Eric's seemingly lucid remarks, his eyes were still not focused.

"I have an idea," Eric said. "Let's build a fire. I have a lighter in my pocket."

"I thought you got rid of that stuff," Billy said.

"I just kept the lighter. It's one of my dad's."

"I guess a fire would be all right." Billy looked around. There was no way for the smoke to escape, so they'd have to build it at the entrance and hope the wind didn't blow the smoke inside and suffocate them. "Let me see what I can find to burn. You just sit here."

Billy gathered several pieces of broken timber, then set out to find some kindling. It was useless. The small shrubs he found beneath the drift at the entrance of the mine had become wet from melting snow and were now refreezing. With no kindling, the tiny lighter would never light the larger pieces of wood. He glanced hopelessly at the snowmobile, wondering if he should try to get it upright and ride for help, but he knew he couldn't. The machine was far too heavy and daylight too far gone. Besides, a rock had punched a hole in the gas tank, and some of the gas had leaked out.

"Now what am I supposed to do?" Billy asked aloud as he started back into the mine. Then he turned and stared at the snowmobile.

He hurried back to the mine. "Eric, I have a plan!"

"Mmmm," Eric said, lifting his head from the rock he was using as a pillow. "What's that hammering?"

Billy bit his lip to keep from crying. He pulled off his coat and shirt, then ripped off his T-shirt and put the other two items back on.

"One hundred percent cotton. Good old Mom," he said. "No polyester. It'll hold the gas and will burn great! You hear that, Eric? I'm gonna get a fire started."

He cleared as much of the debris from the entrance as he could, then scooped together a sort of fireplace with the surrounding dirt. Two boards still held together by rusty nails served as a windbreak at one side of the opening. He carefully stacked the smaller pieces of dry timber from inside the cave into a pile around a bigger log. Grabbing his T-shirt, he raced down the hill to the snowmobile and shoved a torn corner of the sleeve into the hole in the gas tank. He rocked the heavy vehicle to slosh the gas upward, and the cotton shirt absorbed the liquid.

Out of breath, Billy limped back to the cave and stuck the gas-soaked cloth under the pile of wood.

"Quick, gimme the lighter," he said to Eric.

Eric grinned at him and handed it to him. "Sure."

Billy knelt to light the fire, then glanced at his gas-covered gloves. He pulled them off and tossed them out of the way.

"God, I promise I'll always wear my gloves, just like Mom tells me to, if You'll just let me get a fire started."

Trembling with cold, he snapped the lighter top, quickly stepping back, away from the instantaneous fire. Flames immediately ignited the T-shirt, and soon the logs began to hiss and blaze. Billy slumped to the ground beside Eric in relief. At least they wouldn't freeze to death!

— Seventeen —

BILLY LEANED BACK against the dirt wall of the mine, cradling Eric against his shoulder so they could share body heat. As much as he wanted to keep Eric talking, it seemed best to let him sleep. The bump on Eric's forehead was turning black and blue, but the cut had stopped bleeding. Billy had used snow to scrub some of the blood out of his handkerchief, then made a snowball-ice pack that he held against the bump until his fingers became numb.

The large log at the center of the fire seemed to be burning well, but since he would have to keep adding smaller pieces of timber, he didn't dare go to sleep. He felt too hungry and too afraid to sleep anyway.

Eric seemed awfully limp. If it weren't for the irregular lifting of his chest . . . Billy couldn't let himself think such thoughts. Eric was the best friend he'd ever had—the only real friend his own age. He just had to be okay!

Billy nibbled one of the candy bars he'd brought, but that only served to make him hungrier. Though it made him feel guilty and selfish, he ate the second one, reasoning that Eric had thrown up and wouldn't want to eat it anyway.

Outside the small cave, the wind whipped around the hills and spun the snow into deep drifts. The two-board barricade was reinforced by a deepening drift that began to spread across the entrance of the mine.

Billy moved Eric closer to the fire and placed a few more pieces of wood on it. It was going to be a long night. What would Buck do if he were here?

Buck! What a great dad! Billy still couldn't believe that his football hero was really his very own father! Sometimes he thought he should pinch himself to see if it was all a dream. It hadn't started out that way. Just a few months ago he'd wanted Buck to suffer for leaving Billy and his mother alone for so many years. Now he couldn't remember why he'd been so angry. After all, Buck had come around to make things right.

Billy laughed at himself for being so stupid when Buck first showed up. Of course he was his dad. They looked just alike. And why else would a rich and famous quarterback suddenly show up on the doorstep of a dumpy trailer in Colorado? Billy sat back, rested his head against the dirt cave wall, and smiled. What a neat dad he had. He was the best quarterback in the country, in the world! He'd led his team all the way to the playoffs, and he would have won the Super Bowl too if . . .

Billy sighed. There it was again. That awful guilt. It was his fault Buck had been injured. He had sat in his trailer last winter watching the playoff game and had wished Buck would get hurt—hurt bad! And it had happened! Buck wouldn't let him say it. He wouldn't even let him talk about it. And Billy knew how much it hurt Buck that Joey Jones was the one who won the Super Bowl. Joey was okay, but Buck was the one who had made the team what it was. Billy had heard one sportscaster say that every team had a team personality, a special team attitude, and that for the Mavericks that personality was Buck's—hard-driving and tough, but all-around decent.

Buck was the one who had worked for years to pull the Mavericks together. Joey had just copied him to win those last two games. Without Buck they wouldn't be the team they were. Billy hoped Buck could come back next season and take the Mavericks to the Super Bowl again. If there was just something Billy could do to make that happen . . . Just as he'd wished for

Buck to be hurt, could he *wish* him to the Super Bowl? Or better still, should he talk to God about it?

He cleared his throat. He'd never really prayed before, even though his mom and Frankie did it all the time. The way Buck used to do. Why didn't Buck pray anymore or talk to him about the Lord?

Eric groaned and sighed deeply, rolling his head to the side. His eyes fluttered for a moment, and in the flickering light of the fire, he took on a ghostly appearance.

"God, please make Eric be okay." Billy was frightened again for his friend, and the words just popped out.

Eric seemed to settle down again, and Billy sighed with relief.

"Wow," he said. "That really works. Thanks, God. He's my best friend, You know. Please don't let him . . ." Billy paused, shuddering. "Please make him well."

He cocked his head in surprise. This praying stuff was easier than he'd thought.

"And while we're talking, God, could I please ask You something else? I know it's my fault that Buck, I mean, my dad, didn't get to play in the Super Bowl. Please let him play in the next one. Please let the Mavericks win the championship again with him in charge this time."

Billy thought for a moment. "I guess I ought to tell You I'm sorry about wishing he'd get hurt, even dead. You know how sorry I am. You know I . . . umm, I *hated* him. That was wrong. Buck forgave me, so would You please forgive me too? Oh, and God, I want to tell You . . . I . . . I believe in You, just like Gracie did that day in the diner. That was really cool. I guess what I mean is . . . I want to be a Christian, if that's okay with You."

Somehow that seemed to settle things. Billy relaxed for the first time since the snowmobile accident and sat back to watch the snow blowing across the entrance to the mine. The smoke from the fire was starting to cloud the cave, so he carefully laid Eric against the wall, then kicked and pushed away the drift that had accumulated.

Eric sat up, groaning and shivering, and held his head in his hands. "I'm freezing," he mumbled.

Billy knelt by his friend. "I'm freezing too. Maybe we'd better get up and walk around to get warm." He started to drag Eric to his feet, but his friend resisted.

"My head hurts. I want to lie down."

"Look, you can't lie down and get warm too. Let's walk around for a while, then we can rest again, okay? Take a few whiffs of this clean Colorado air my mom is always bragging about."

After a few deep breaths, Eric allowed Billy to help him stand up. Wobbling for a moment, he nodded. "Okay, let's take a hike."

The two boys began walking in a circle, leaning against each other.

"Man," Billy said, "I've lived in Colorado all my life, and I've never been this cold."

"You think this is cold." Eric winced as he spoke but forced himself to go on. "Let me tell you about Switzerland."

Led by Terrell Martin's truck, two other giant eighteen-wheelers and several four-wheel drive vehicles pulled off the highway onto the side road that wound gradually around the hills to the movie location. As they pulled into the parking area, Janice saw Bill throw open his trailer door and race toward them. She jumped from Terrell's truck and flung herself into his arms.

"Oh, Bill, Bill . . ."

"Janice, I'm so sorry . . ."

"It's not your fault." Janice was surprised at her own words, but they were true. Just as it hadn't been her fault when Billy fell from the train tracks three years before, it was not Bill's fault their son had picked a bad time to wander away from the movie set.

"I want so badly to say it's going to be all right," he said, "but I can't."

She shivered both from the cold and from his ominous words. "I know."

"I'm really scared, Janice." Bill held her tightly.

"Me, too." His strong arms provided the first measure of comfort she'd felt for hours.

Terrell Martin and his friend Stacey, along with all the other volunteers, got out of their vehicles and surrounded the couple.

"What can we do to help?" Terrell said.

Bill stared at the truck driver, his would-be rival. The man's expression was as sincere as his tone of voice.

"The sheriff is directing the search. You can ask him. He's over there." Bill pointed to several official trucks and all-terrain vehicles parked nearby. "Thanks for coming, Martin."

Terrell nodded, touching the rim of his cowboy hat. "Glad to." Then he and the others went to offer their services to the sheriff.

"Can't we search too?" Janice asked. "Why aren't you looking? I'm sorry—I shouldn't have said that."

"It's okay. Rob and I did go out for a while. But the sheriff sent us back here. These people know what they're doing, and the last thing they need is a couple of frantic, city-bred fathers getting lost too. I'm sorry—I guess that sounds pretty lame. But these guys are the experts."

He led her back to the trailer and offered her some hot chocolate. "Let's keep our strength up, okay?"

He sat beside her on the couch with his arm around her.

Relaxing into his embrace, Janice held the cup of cocoa and let her fingers absorb its warmth. "Where's Rob?"

"He was here but went back to his trailer. He'll probably be back soon. He's pacing all over the place."

She stared at him. "I'm surprised you're not pacing."

He grunted. "Yeah, me too." He was quiet for a moment. "Janice, something happened this afternoon that I want to tell you about. I was starting to call you when I found out the boys were missing."

As he looked down into her eyes, his heart ached over the pain he saw. Their son was missing and might not be found alive. Once again Bill winced as he thought of his failure to lead his family spiritually. Could he ever forgive himself if Billy died without coming to know Jesus as his Savior? With a shuddering half-sob, he pulled Janice close and kissed her forehead.

Janice set her cup down and returned his embrace, hoping he drew as much comfort from her closeness as she did from his. "So tell me."

"It was the scene we shot today. Man, was it just today? It seems so long ago. Anyway, I had to do a prayer. Do? Yeah, that's exactly what it seemed like. Then Rob, of all people, told me to play it like I was talking to God as though He's a real person. Janice, I've been so wrong. I've been so angry with God about the Super Bowl that I've completely failed you and Billy. But when I said that prayer for my movie character, I realized that I wanted to be back in fellowship with God. I want to talk to Him because He *is* a real person. I came back here to the trailer after we shot the scene, and I got right with God. I told Him I was sorry for being so stupid. I have what's really important—you and Billy."

"Oh, Bill . . ." Janice struggled to talk through her tears. "I'm so thankful . . . I was so confused . . . I didn't understand why you didn't want to pray . . . I know you want to play football, but we just want *you*."

"We can live wherever you want to, Janice."

"That place you showed me in the San Fernando Valley is beautiful . . ."

"I've played enough football. I can find another career . . ."

"Not until you win that stupid Super Bowl next year!"

"We can have another baby. I'd love another kid . . ."

Janice gasped, then broke down in sobs. "I . . . just . . . want . . . Billy . . . back . . . safe!"

Rob Ruskin jerked the door open, knocking on it as he entered the trailer. "Buck, I think . . . Oh, I'm sorry. Hello,

Janice. I should have known you were here—all those trucks out there and everything... More people searching... Something's bound to happen soon." He turned back toward the door in confusion.

"Come on in, Rob," Bill said. He stroked Janice's hair as her sobs subsided. "Sit down awhile. You look beat."

Ruskin dropped into an easy chair and leaned forward. "Listen, is it my imagination or did the snow slow up some about the same time . . . I mean, after we . . . a while ago after we p-prayed?" He could barely make himself say the word.

"I don't know. I haven't been outside except when Janice got here," Bill said. "But now that you mention it, it has slowed up."

Janice sat up and dried her tears with the handkerchief Bill offered. "As we came over La Veta Pass, we noticed it was lighter on this side than we'd expected." She sniffed and blew her nose.

Ruskin was out of his chair again. "I'm going to check. Come outside a minute. See what you think."

The trio stepped from the trailer into the icy cold of the night as the last feathery flakes of snow were settling to the ground. High in the northern sky, stars burst through the deep darkness of space and twinkled like diamonds. As though mirroring the heavenly light show, the great black mountains danced with the lights of a hundred searchers.

"Now is when it really gets cold," Janice said.

Ruskin frowned. "How could it get any colder?"

"It isn't as cold when it's snowing," she explained. "But after the cloud cover is gone, the temperature can get real low. It's 50 below up here a lot of the time. Even in the summer a person can freeze to death in these mountains . . ." As she talked, her tone grew more desperate.

"Janice . . ." Bill held her close and put his finger on her lips. "Shhh," he said softly. How he wanted to comfort her! But his own heart ached as much as hers did.

He stared back at the dancing pinpoints of light on the mountains. Higher and far to the right of the main body, a larger light glowed more brightly than the rest. One of the searchers must have become detached from the others. In fact, the light actually seemed to flicker. Had someone started a fire up there so the searchers could warm themselves? Or could it be . . . ?

"Janice, would you go get me some more hot chocolate? I want to ask the sheriff something." He didn't want to give her false hope.

"Hey, is that . . . ?" Ruskin said, his eyes focusing on the same flaring light.

"What is it?" Janice followed their line of vision. "Bill, that's a fire! That could be the boys!"

Racing across the lot to the sheriff's truck, the three parents babbled at once to the uniformed officer.

"Do you see that big light?"

"Is that a fire?"

"That could be my son."

The sheriff leaned casually against the truck, tapping his pipe against his boot. He pulled a pouch from his pocket and packed the pipe for another smoke.

"Could be," he drawled.

"Well, why aren't you up there checking it out?" shouted Ruskin.

The sheriff sniffed, took a draw on his pipe, and eyed the actor up and down. "Got a chopper on the way." In one fluid movement, he nodded curtly to Ruskin, smiled at Bill, and winked at Janice, then sauntered away toward a group of returning searchers.

"I don't need to be on this thing," Billy complained from his stretcher. "I can walk."

"Just lie still, son," the paramedic said. "We're going to take you for a little ride down to the hospital in that ambulance over there and check you over. That left leg is bruised and swollen."

"Oh, Billy," cried Janice as she knelt beside him and caressed his face.

"Aw, Mom, cut that out. I'm fine," he said. "It's Eric I'm worried about."

"He's okay, son," Bill said. "The helicopter took him to the hospital in Pueblo. Rob went with him. He probably has a concussion and might need a few stitches, but he's going to be all right." He knelt beside Janice. "I'm proud of you, Billy. You got that fire started. And you probably saved Eric's life."

"Awww." Billy wrinkled his nose, then grinned. "Really?"

"What I want to know," the paramedic said, "is how you knew to keep him awake and walking around. Did you recognize the symptoms of a concussion?"

Billy's face showed his confusion. "No. I don't know nothing, eh, anything about that stuff. We were just trying to keep warm." He frowned, thinking hard. "But I think it was right after I prayed that it seemed like a good idea. Hey, Mom, I decided to be a Christian too. I had a cool talk with God." He looked doubtfully at Bill. "Is that okay, Buck?"

Janice squeaked out a delighted "Oh!" and leaned forward to give her son a hug.

But Bill turned away, hanging his head and running his hands through his hair. God had saved Billy in spite of his father's failures. Surely He could be trusted with everything else—where they lived, football, the Super Bowl—*everything!*

"Dad?" Billy said softly. "Is that okay?"

Bill took a deep breath to keep from sobbing, but then as he turned back to his son he decided not to hide his tears. He smiled and stepped back to the gurney, holding out his hand for a lowered version of a high five. "Yeah, son," he said. "That's okay. In fact, that's downright terrific!"

Billy smiled back at his father as he reached up to slap his hand. For once Buck's tears didn't make him uncomfortable, or his mother's either. He looked beyond his parents at the old man hanging back from the happy family reunion.

"Hey, Pops," he called out to his newly found grandfather. "Come on over here."

Albert Griffin shuffled uncertainly toward them. "I . . . I don't want to butt in."

"You're not butting in," Billy said. "Is he, Mom? Hey, Mom, isn't it cool for both of us to have a dad after all these years?"

Janice studied Billy's face. He'd only been saved a few short hours, but God's love was already reflected in his eyes as he looked at her and then over her shoulder. She followed his gaze and found herself staring into the face of her father. His shoulders were slumped just like Peter's had been when his girlfriend had broken up with him. His head was cocked in the same boyish way. His lonely, sorrowful Peter-like eyes melted the last remnants of bitterness in her heart. He was family—but could she accept him? Surely if Billy could not only forgive but love and accept Bill despite his once deserting them, she could do the same for her own father. Surely if God could love and accept her and give her living proof of it through her new Christian friends, she couldn't refuse to love and accept this man who needed it so desperately.

She stood up and stepped over to Hal, looping her arms through his and Bill's, then gazed down at her son.

"Yes, it sure is, honey. It's the coolest!"

6.00